SEEK THE STARS

In the late eighteenth century The Marchioness of Langbourne tells the Earl of Kensall that her husband has put a Detective on them, and has threatened to divorce her and cite the Earl as co-respondent. He is desperate at the thought of a scandal and that traditionally he will have to live abroad for at least five years and then be obliged to marry the Marchioness.

The Marchioness however, has a solution. The Earl is aghast when he hears it, but accepts that it is the only way out of the situation.

The Marchioness has told her husband that it was his daughter Sadira whom the Earl has been seeing and who intends to ask his permission to marry her. Using various cruel threats the Marchioness convinces her Stepdaughter that it would be in her best interests to marry the Earl, and she reluctantly agrees.

As the days pass however, she realises it is for her an untenable position and when the opportunity to escape presents itself, she grasps it. But the Earl realises she is in danger and goes in search of her.

How, by rescuing a little child she unites two peoples, and how the Earl saves Sadira from certain death, is all told in this delightful story, the 482nd by Barbara Cartland.

SEEK THE STARS

Barbara Cartland

SEVERN HOUSE PUBLISHERS

W.S.C.

This first world edition published in Great Britain 1991 by
SEVERN HOUSE PUBLISHERS LTD of
35 Manor Road, Wallington, Surrey SM6 0BW
Simultaneously first published in the U.S.A. 1991 by
SEVERN HOUSE PUBLISHERS INC. of
475 Fifth Avenue, New York, NY 10017-6220

British Library Cataloguing in Publication Data

Cartland, Barbara, *1902 –*
  Seek The Stars
  823.914

  ISBN 0-7278-4225-0

Printed and bound in Great Britain by
Billing and Sons Ltd, Worcester

AUTHOR'S NOTE

Mankind has been entranced, fascinated and inspired by stars since the beginning of Civilisation. The Star of Bethlehem was symbolic of the human search not only for Faith, but for Love.

Today nearly every newspaper has columns on the stars, to guide people according to their birth date. Personally I put very little faith in these. as it is very complicated to work out how exactly the time one is born can be interpreted by the stars.

Most of the Astrologers, in my opinion, are wrong in what they predict.

For instance, Napoleon Bonaparte used Astrologers and so did Hitler. Neither of them were told it would be disastrous to go to Russia, and if they did go, to leave before the winter started in September.

Napoleon lost half of his Army, not to the Russian guns, but to the weather.

I can still remember the film that was shown of 150,000 of Hitler's soldiers being taken prisoner, shivering in their summer uniforms. The tanks and guns were grounded because the petrol and the oil were frozen.

Today the Japanese use the stars continually, not only for personal advice but also in their monetary investments on the Stock Exchange. But their Astrologers never told them that Pearl Harbour would eventually lead to Hiroshima.

At the same time, the fascination of the stars will go on.

We will believe in our hearts that through the stars we will find the perfect love which, whether we admit it or not, all human beings seek, and which a few are privileged to find.

ABOUT THE AUTHOR

Barbara Cartland, the world's most famous romantic novelist, who is also an historian, playwright, lecturer, political speaker and television personality, has now written over 500 books and sold over 500 million copies all over the world.

She has also had many historical works published and has written four autobiographies as well as the biographies of her mother and that of her brother, Ronald Cartland, who was the first Member of Parliament to be killed in the last war. This book has a preface by Sir Winston Churchill and has just been republished with an introduction by the late Sir Arthur Bryant.

"Love at the Helm" a novel written with the help and inspiration of the late Earl Mountbatten of Burma, Great Uncle of His Royal Highness The Prince of Wales, is being sold for the Mountbatten Memorial Trust.

She has broken the world record for the last thirteen years by writing an average of twenty-three books a year. In the Guiness Book of Records she is listed as the world's top-selling author.

Miss Cartland in 1978 sang an Album of Love Songs with the Royal Philharmonic Orchestra.

In private life Barbara Cartland, who is a Dame of Grace of the Order of St. John of Jerusalem, Chairman of the St. John Council in Hertfordshire and Deputy President of the St. John Ambulance Brigade, has fought for better conditions and salaries for Midwives and Nurses.

She championed the cause for the Elderly in 1956 invoking a Government Enquiry into the "Housing Conditions of Old People".

In 1962 she had the Law of England changed so that Local Authorities had to provide camps for their own Gypsies. This has meant that since then thousands and thousands of Gypsy children have been able to go to School which they had never been able to do in the past, as their caravans were moved every twenty-four hours by the Police.

There are now fourteen camps in Hertfordshire and Barbara Cartland has her own Romany Gypsy Camp called Barbaraville by the Gypsies.

Her designs "Decorating with Love" are being sold all over the U.S.A. and the National Home Fashions League made her, in 1981, "Woman of Achievement".

Barbara Cartland's book "Getting Older, Growing Younger" has been published in Great Britain and the U.S.A. and her fifth Cookery Book, "The Romance of Food", is now being used by the House of Commons.

In 1984 she received at Kennedy Airport, America's Bishop Wright Air Industry Award for her contribution to the development of aviation. In 1931 she and two R.A.F. Officers thought of, and carried, the first aeroplane-towed glider air-mail.

During the War she was Chief Lady Welfare Officer in Bedfordshire looking after 20,000 Service men and women. She thought of having a pool of Wedding Dresses at the War Office so a Service Bride could hire a gown for the day.

She bought 1,000 secondhand gowns without coupons for the A.T.S., the W.A.A.F.s and the W.R.E.N.S. In 1945 Barbara Cartland received the Certificate of Merit from Eastern Command.

In 1964 Barbara Cartland founded the National Association for Health of which she is the President, as a front for all the Health Stores and for any product made as alternative medicine.

This has now a £500,000,000 turnover a year, with one third going in export.

In January 1988 she received "La Medaille de Vermeil de la Ville de Paris", (the Gold Medal of Paris). This is the highest award to be given by the City of Paris for ACHIEVEMENT – 25 million books sold in France.

In March 1988 Barbara Cartland was asked by the Indian Government to open their Health Resort outside Delhi. This is almost the largest Health Resort in the world.

Barbara Cartland was received with great enthusiasm by her fans, who also fêted her at a Reception in the city and she received the gift of an embossed plate from the Government.

OTHER BOOKS BY
BARBARA CARTLAND

Romantic Novels, over 490, the most recently published being:

Just Fate	Born of Love
A Miracle in Mexico	The Angel and The Rake
Warned by a Ghost	The Queen of Hearts
Terror from the Throne	The Wicked Widow
The Cave of Love	To Scotland and Love
The Peaks of Ecstasy	Love and War
A Kiss in Rome	Love at The Ritz
Hidden by Love	The Dangerous Marriage
Walking to Wonderland	Good or Bad
Lucky Logan Finds Love	This is Love

The Dream and the Glory (In aid of the St. John Ambulance Brigade)

Autobiographical and Biographical:

The Isthmus Years 1919–1939
The Years of Opportunity 1939–1945
I Search for Rainbows 1945–1976
We Danced All Night 1919–1929
Ronald Cartland (With a foreword by Sir Winston Churchill)

Polly – My Wonderful Mother
I Seek the Miraculous

Historical:

Bewitching Women
The Outrageous Queen (The Story of Queen Christina of
    Sweden)
The Scandalous Life of King Carol
The Private Life of Charles II
The Private Life of Elizabeth, Empress of Austria
Josephine, Empress of France
Diane de Poitiers
Metternich – The Passionate Diplomat
A Year of Royal Days
Royal Jewels
Royal Eccentrics
Royal Lovers.

Sociology:

You in the Home
The Fascinating Forties
Marriage for Moderns
Be Vivid, Be Vital
Love, Life and Sex
Vitamins for Vitality
Husbands and Wives
Men are Wonderful
Etiquette
The Many Facets of Love
Sex and the Teenager
The Book of Charm
Living Together
The Youth Secret
The Magic of Honey
The Book of Beauty and
    Health
Keep Young and Beautiful by Barbara Cartland and Elinor
    Glyn

Etiquette for Love and Romance
Barbara Cartland's Book of Health

General:

Barbara Cartland's Book of Useless Information with a
  Foreword by the Earl Mountbatten of Burma.
  (In aid of the United World Colleges)
Love and Lovers (Picture Book)
The Light of Love (Prayer Book)
Barbara Cartland's Scrapbook
  (In aid of the Royal Photographic Museum)
Romantic Royal Marriages
Barbara Cartland's Book of Celebrities
Getting Older, Growing Younger

Verse:

Lines on Life and Love

Music:

An album of Love Songs sung with the Royal Philharmonic Orchestra.

Films:

The Flame is Love
A Hazard of Hearts
The Lady and The Highwayman

Cartoons:

Barbara Cartland Romances (Book of Cartoons) has recently
  been published in the U.S.A., Great Britain, and other
  parts of the world.

Children:

A Children's Pop-Up Book: "Princess to the Rescue"

Videos:

A Hazard of Hearts
The Lady and The Highwayman

Cookery:

Barbara Cartland's Health Food Cookery Book
Food for Love
Magic of Honey Cookbook
Recipes for Lovers
The Romance of Food

Editor of:

"The Common Problem" by Ronald Cartland (with a
  preface by the Rt. Hon. the Earl of Selborne, P.C.)
Barbara Cartland's Library of Love
                    Library of Ancient Wisdom
"Written with Love" Passionate love letters selected by Barbara
  Cartland

Drama:

Blood Money
French Dressing

Philosophy:

Touch the Stars

Radio Operetta:

The Rose and the Violet (Music by Mark Lubbock)
Performed in 1942.

Radio Plays:

The Caged Bird: An episode in the life of Elizabeth
Empress of Austria Performed in 1957.

CHAPTER ONE

The Earl of Kensall came down the stairs to breakfast at precisely eight o'clock. His years of training in the Army had made him a very punctual man, and he disliked being late himself, or being kept waiting by anybody else.

It would have been impossible for anyone looking at him not to be impressed, for he was over six feet tall, with square shoulders and was beyond dispute extremely handsome.

Ever since he had been a boy he had been acclaimed for his good looks, and women had fallen into his arms even before he asked their names.

He was not particularly conceited.

He was just aware of his own importance and determined that his way of life should be one of dignity. As the head of a large family he was looked up to and revered. They turned to him for advice, and when they received it, carried it out to the letter. His possessions, including his large estate in the country, were run in a methodical manner which made him the envy of every other Landlord.

The Earl was now nearly thirty, but in many ways he was older than his years. He was extremely intelligent, and when he spoke in the House of Lords he always had an attentive audience. Indeed, the Prime Minister and other leading Statesmen were known to consult him regularly, especially on matters in which the national interest was concerned.

The extraordinary thing was that despite his many *affaires de coeur* he had not yet married.

Naturally his older relations were continually begging him to do so. "You must realise, Norwin," they said, "that you need an heir, with several younger brothers in reserve, to make sure of the succession."

The Earl knew that their anxiety rested on the fact that his father had had only one child, namely himself. The whole family had been terrified that while he was serving in the Army he might be killed. The fact that he had survived was in part due to his habitual good luck which was the envy of all his friends, and he was well aware that the Betting-Book at White's Club recorded a number of wagers about him, including whether he would be married before the end of the year, or whether one of the more determined of the ambitious Mamas would capture him to the humiliation of the others.

He had, however, managed deftly to avoid a great many traps and remained a bachelor. Older members of the Jockey Club, with whom he was closely associated on every racecourse, had often, as a last resort, approached him.

First they would congratulate him on his horse being first past the winning-post. Then they would comment on what a magnificent stallion he had and would exclaim "As I have some excellent mares it seems a pity that we do not breed a champion between us!"

"It is certainly an idea," the Earl would murmur.

Then came the inevitable invitation.

"Why not come down to stay for a few days and see what I have to offer? Incidentally, my eldest daughter, who is just eighteen, is extremely beautiful."

The Earl was aware that this was yet another trap and would decline tactfully.

Now he crossed the Hall to the Breakfast-Room, which was considerably smaller than the Dining-Room. For Kensall House in Park Lane had been in the family for two generations, while Kensall Park in Hampshire had been in the possession of the Earls of Kensall for nearly four hundred years, and it had been altered considerably by generation after generation. The present Earl's Grandfather who was the sixth in succession, had made it more comfortable and more luxurious than it had ever been before, and the present Earl had added extensively to the Picture Gallery.

He had a taste for Art which had not been noticeable among his antecedents, and was now thinking whether he should buy a very fine picture by Holbein, which had been offered to him by its owner before being put up for sale at Christie's. It would certainly be a magnificent addition to his collection, but the Earl had a feeling that if he bought it privately it might cost him more than if he bid for it in the Sale Room.

The Butler had timed him to the minute. As His Lordship entered the Breakfast-Room he came in at the other door, carrying in the coffee-pot which he set down on the silver tray at the top of the table. He then placed beside it the day's editions of *The Times* and the *Morning Post*.

Without speaking the Earl walked across the room to the sideboard. Exquisitely carved and gilded, it supported six silver entree dishes kept hot by oil-wicks burning underneath each one.

There was a different variety of dishes to choose from each morning, and as the Earl was ready to help himself the Butler left the room and he was alone. He raised the lids of each of the entree dishes and finally took a plateful of salmon with fresh mushrooms, which had been brought the previous day from Kensall Park.

It gave him a feeling of pleasure to know that he was eating his own home produce rather than what had come from a shop. Indeed he wondered if the salmon had come from the river which flowed through his own land. Though occasionally a salmon was to be found in it, it was, however, more likely to provide him with trout such as he had eaten for dinner the previous evening.

Having served himself he went to his place at the top of the table and sat down and opened his copy of *The Times* at the page which was usually devoted to European affairs. He was particularly interested in the confrontation which was taking place at the moment between France and Germany regarding the price of sheep. He propped up the newspaper on a silver stand, and as he ate his breakfast he read what was happening.

He had just finished the salmon and was wondering whether he should sample one of the other dishes when the door opened. The Butler came in and crossed the room to his Master's side.

"What is it, Duncan?" the Earl asked in a slightly irritated tone, for he disliked anybody disturbing or talking to him while he was having breakfast.

"Excuse me, M'Lord," Duncan replied, "but a Lady has just called. She says it's extremely important that she should see Your Lordship immediately."

The Earl raised his eyebrows. "A Lady?" he questioned. "Who is she?"

The Butler hesitated. Thinking it best to be frank he replied, "The Lady be heavily veiled, M'Lord, but I'm almost sure it's the Marchioness of Langbourne."

The Earl stiffened.

Then he said in a low voice as if he was speaking to himself, "That is impossible!"

The Butler hesitated, then said, "I've shown th' Lady into th' Study, M'Lord, an' she asked me twice to inform Your Lordship how urgent th' matter were."

The Earl put his napkin down on the table and rose to his feet. He did not speak, but was frowning as he walked across the room. As the Butler hurried to open the door he went out into the hall, and walked down the corridor to the Study which was where he habitually sat when he was alone. This was a very attractive room with a long French window opening out onto the garden. The walls were covered with books except where two fine portraits of previous Earls hung, one painted by Van Dyck.

A footman opened the door and the Earl walked in.

He could see now that Duncan was right. It was the Marchioness of Langbourne who was waiting to see him. She had removed what the Butler had described as a heavy veil from her face, and it was now thrown back over her hat.

An exceedingly beautiful woman, she had not at first been publicly acclaimed in the way she was now. The Professional Beauties had come into being owing to the attention they received from the Prince of Wales. The Marchioness had at first escaped his notice, but then His Royal Highness had started including her amongst his intimate circle of friends. The public, informed by the newspapers, hastily appreciated her loveliness, for with her dark hair and a magnolia skin, quite a number of fashionable Artists had asked her to sit for them.

She was also watched for when she drove in the Park, so much so that her husband, the Marquess, had forbidden photographs of her to be published, such as were sold over the counter of the other Beauties. Nevertheless there was a daily clamour at the stationers for photographs of her.

The Marchioness had been elusive where the Prince of Wales was concerned. She made him laugh and flirted with him, and because of her witty conversation she was invariably included in every large party he gave. At the same time she managed, without offending him, to ward off any suggestion that their friendship should be of a more intimate nature.

Then she met the Earl of Kensall.

At the first glance she was aware he was exactly what she had been waiting for. She was, at the age of twenty-six, at the height of her beauty. She was quite confident that any man who received an invitation from her dark blue eyes would find her irresistable.

She was the second wife of the Marquess of Langbourne, who was very much older than she was. In fact, he had celebrated his fiftieth birthday before they met. In this he had more than emulated his predecessor, for the Marchioness's first husband had been over sixty when she married him.

Lord Granton wanted an heir and was looking round for an attractive young woman who would give him one. He was scrutinising the young women in London when quite by chance, when he was at home in his own Country House, he met the daughter of a neighbour.

Daphne Wareham had never thought to contract a marriage of such social consequence. She had of course, heard Lord Granton talked about ever since she was a child. When his wife died there was a great deal of genuine commiseration for him, especially as he was a kindly Landlord who contributed generously to the charities in the County.

Daphne's mother had decided that now she was eighteen she should appear first at the local Hunt Ball and then various other County festivities. She would then go to London the following year for the Season.

"I shall be too old, Mama, to be a débutante." Daphne protested.

"Nonsense!" Mrs. Wareham replied. "You will simply be a little more sophisticated than the other girls and that will be an advantage."

She looked at her daughter before she said, "Of course,

Dearest, you may manage to get married before then. There are quite a lot of attractive young men in the Country."

Daphne had agreed with her. She had actually thought that one young man who was to inherit a Baronetcy would suit her, and whom she had met out hunting.

He would, if he asked her, be exactly the sort of husband she hoped for, and they were already quite friendly. Ye he had not responded to her rather shy hint that he might like to call on her father and see his horses. Then at a garden-party given by Lord Granton as Lord Lieutenant she shone like a star.

Her gown which had been bought for the occasion was certainly somewhat fanciful for a young girl, whilst her hat was trimmed with small feathers instead of the conventional flowers.

Lord Granton now had no wife to support him as he had had in previous years, and he therefore made more of an effort than usual to circulate among his guests. He greeted Daphne's father, Colonel Wareham, with pleasure because he had known him for a long time.

Then the Colonel said, "I do not think you have met my daughter, My Lord."

Lord Granton had looked at Daphne and found it impossible to look away. Most young girls simpered shyly when he addressed them. Their eye-lashes fluttered and they blushed if he paid them a compliment, but Daphne was different.

Her eyes sparkled, and she managed without any difficulty to hold Lord Granton spellbound by everything she had to say.

During the afternoon he invited Colonel Wareham with his wife and Daphne to dinner the following evening.

By the end of the week he was in love.

It was beyond the Warehams' wildest dreams that their daughter should become Lady Granton and wife of the Lord Lieutenant. The disparity in their ages had never even been thought about, let alone commented upon. All anyone could think of was that an ordinary young girl, although her family was an ancient one, was marrying into the aristocracy. Lord Granton was as infatuated as if he were a boy of twenty.

He heaped presents on Daphne.

He gave her a horse such as she had never imagined owning. He also insisted that the marriage should take place as soon as possible.

Her mother took Daphne to London to buy her trousseau, and she was married in the small village church on Lord Granton's estate, where Daphne had been christeened and Lord Granton's first wife was buried.

Showered with rose-petals and rice, they set off on their honeymoon, with the cheers and good wishes of all their friends in the County echoing in their ears. To Daphne it was all unreal, but at the same time exhilarating, being called 'My Lady', and finding herself Chatelaine of the huge house she had looked at with awe ever since she was a small child.

Unfortunately, only a few months after the marriage, Lord Granton had a stroke. For the next two years Daphne sat by his bedside while the Doctors came and went but could do nothing. When at last Lord Granton died it was a merciful release.

And so, after a year of mourning she came to London where she was clever enough to persuade a Lady of Quality, but in straightlaced circumstances, to chaperon her and present her at Court.

Now she had plenty of money and could afford to rent a large house in Mayfair. She was also expensively dressed, and soon attracted attention. For six months she dazzled the most sophisticated society in England before she met the Marquess of Langbourne. Himself recently widowed, unhappy, restless and trying to adjust himself to being alone, he was an easy conquest.

Two months later they were married quietly.

Daphne now thought she had everything she had ever wanted. There was a huge house in the country, a fine house in London and, although she could hardly believe it, she was by tradition a Lady of the Bedchamber to the Queen. She felt then she had reached the height of glory such as she had only read about in history books and novels.

For the first year of their marriage she obeyed her husband and did exactly as he wished. She felt sometimes as she had with Lord Granton, namely that he was rather like a father to her but at other times a rather strict schoolmaster.

Then she began to assert herself, for she soon had very different ideas of what interested her and what she desired from life. She was however in no hurry.

The Marquess after a long honeymoon had come back to an endless series of official duties, which occupied him every day when he was in London. In the country he was also busy with his estates. So, again, as if history was repeating itself, Daphne found herself alone.

She was therefore able to choose her own interests, her own amusements and, more important, her own friends.

These included men.

Men whom she entertained and with whom she danced and flirted.

Because she was intelligent she was careful not to neglect her husband in any way, but when she took her first lover she was terrified. She had been afraid of her reputation when she was widowed, now she was frightened in case the Marquess should somehow suspect that she was being unfaithful to him.

The Marquess was often very tired in the evening. Also he was so busy during the day that as long as he could see his wife at the end of the dining-table he was happy. Yet, he did not realise that she was coming into bloom like a rose. As a woman rather than a girl she now required more attention.

She was however terrified of doing anything that would damage her socially. Daphne therefore had amorous affairs with unimportant young men who remained unnoticed by the gossips.

Only occasionally was the Marquess slightly jealous, but she laughed at his suspicions.

"I want only you to admire me, my Darling. But if other men do so, then that is a compliment to you."

She revelled in becoming a public beauty and she was delighted by the admiration she evoked and the publicity she received in the newspapers and magazines.

Then she met the Earl.

For the first time in her life Daphne fell in love.

The Earl of Kensall was a very much more ardent lover than anybody she had known before. He was what she had always craved for – a conqueror. Until now, she had secretly despised the men who pleaded for her favours.

The Earl, like "a Monarch of all he surveyed", swept her off her feet. He made her surrender to him and took it for granted that he would capture her heart, and assumed she would fall wildly and inescapably in love with him. He gave her sensations she had never known before, and when he left her she counted the hours until she could see him again.

Now when he came into the room where she was waiting she was aware that he was very angry. He was angry that she should have done anything so indiscreet as to call on him so early in the day.

The Earl shut the door behind him, then said in a sharp voice, "Daphne! What are you doing here?"

"I had to . . . come! I had to . . . see you. Norwin!" she cried. "Something terrible . . . ghastly . . . devastating . . . has happened!"

There was no doubt that she was agitated and the Earl thought that to reveal it was a mistake. He had no wish for the servants to talk, for he fondly believed that his *affaires de coeur*, and there were a great number of them, were not of interest in the Servants' Hall.

He walked slowly towards the Marchioness, and appeared not to notice that she put out her ungloved hands towards him.

"What has happened?" he demanded. "You know as

well as I do that it is a mistake for you to call at this hour."

"I know, I know!" Daphne admitted. "But I had to see you, and this was the . . . only way I could do so. Arthur thinks I am in Church."

The Earl looked surprised.

"Arthur?" he repeated. "Are you saying that he has returned?"

"He came back . . . unexpectedly last night," the Marchioness replied. "As you know, I thought he would be away for . . . another week, but he . . . returned because he has had me . . . watched."

The Earl was startled.

There was silence before he said in a voice that he found hard to recognise as his own:

"Did you say – he has had you watched?"

"Y.yes," Daphne said with a little sob. "He set a Detective on me before he went away to France, and when he received the man's report he came back without telling anybody what he was doing."

The Earl thought it was indeed fortunate that he had not visited Daphne last night. He had attended his Regimental Dinner and when it was over it was very late and he was tired. He had been with her the night before and the night before that.

Almost as if he followed his thoughts, Daphne said: "I was asleep in bed and, of course, alone when Arthur came in. He raged at me, telling me that he had a Detective's report of all my movements since he had left England."

The Earl drew in his breath. He knew that if this was true he was heavily involved in what could turn out to be an appalling scandal.

Daphne sank down on the sofa and put her hands up to her eyes. "He read out the report which included all the times when you came to the house and when . . . you left."

The Earl thought he had been extremely stupid, for he should have realised there was a man watching him when he left, especially as on some occasions this had been after dawn had broken.

Before he could ask the question, Daphne said in a broken voice, "Arthur . . . says he . . . intends to . . . divorce me!"

"I do not believe it!" the Earl exclaimed.

"He says . . . that is what he . . . intends to do . . . and you know how . . . obstinate he is and how it is . . . impossible to make him . . . change his . . . mind."

"But you tried – for God's sake say you tried!" the Earl insisted.

As he spoke he thought with horror of the position he was in. A suit for divorce, which was a very difficult thing to obtain, would have to go through the House of Lords, and every word of the action would be published in the newspapers.

What was more, it meant, before the Marquess obtained his divorce, there would be many months of negotiations between the Lawyers.

If the Marquess was successful, as undoubtedly he would be, he, as a Gentleman, would have to ask Daphne to be his wife.

They would then be expected to go abroad, and it would be at least five years before it was possible for them to return to England.

Even then, while he would be more or less accepted in men's Society, Daphne would be ostracised for the rest of her life. No Social Hostess would permit her to cross her threshold, and they would be confined to knowing only the "Rag-Tag and Bobtail", who were people like themselves who had caused an unforgivable scandal, or people who were prepared to go anywhere and know anyone for a free drink.

To the Earl it seemed as if he was facing a hell on earth. He thought he would rather die than spend the rest of his life living like that.

"Surely you argued with him?" he said at length, his voice seeming to come from a long distance away.

"I not only . . . argued with him," Daphne replied, "I told him it was . . . not true."

"Did you expect him to believe that?"

"I told him," Daphne said, "that when you came to the house it was . . . not to see me . . . but Sadira."

The Earl stared at her.

For a moment he could not think what she meant.

Then he remembered that the Marquess had a daughter by his previous marriage, and he had seen her once disappearing down the end of a corridor. Now he thought of it, he might have met her at an "At Home" which her Stepmother had given. This would have been early in their acquaintance when he was still no more than curious about Daphne, and he had no memory now what the girl had looked like.

"I do not think he is any more likely to believe that!" he said.

"I told him," Daphne explained, "that . . . now he had

come home you would be calling to . . . ask for Sadira's .
. . hand . . . in . . . marriage."

As she said the words they seemed to tremble on her
lips.

"Marry her?" he said sharply. "How can I marry a girl I
have never spoken to or even met?"

"But you have to . . . do you not see? You . . . have
to!" Daphne said desperately. "And that is what I have
come to . . . tell you. I do not think Arthur really believes
. . . you are interested . . . in Sadira, but however much
he may threaten me with . . . a divorce . . . he will not . . .
want a social . . . scandal."

"I am sure . . ." the Earl began.

"Listen, you must listen!" Daphne said urgently. "He
will accept you as his son-in-law simply because you are
so important . . . and that is the . . . only way we can save
. . . ourselves."

She threw out her hands as she went on:

"You know what Arthur is like – or perhaps you do
not. He is above all, extremely proud. He cannot bear to
think you have made a fool of him."

She paused a moment and then went on, "The only
way by which we can save ourselves is for you to marry
Sadira, and Arthur can save his own face at the . . . same
time."

The Earl stared at Daphne as if he could not believe
what she was saying. He tried to protest that it was quite
impossible and the whole idea was ridiculous; yet he
found the words would not leave his lips.

He could see vaguely, like the light at the end of a very
dark tunnel, that in fact this might be the way out. It

would be however at a cost to himself which was utterly and completely intolerable.

He walked across the room to the window, and looked out with unseeing eyes at the sunshine that bathed the garden.

"There *must* be some other way," he said at last.

"No! There is none! I lay awake the rest of the night, after Arthur had raged at me until three o'clock. He called me appalling names which is something he has never done before."

She drew in her breath before she went on, "You must see, Norwin, that it has been a terrible shock to him. He is old, but he likes to think of himself as young. He has sometimes been a little jealous but has always believed that I was absolutely and completely faithful."

Without turning round the Earl said, "You have been extremely clever in the past. Surely you can do something now?"

"I *have* done something, and that is what I came here to tell you." Daphne insisted. "When he returned last night he was determined to throw me out of the house and start divorce proceedings against me citing you as co-respondent."

She gave a deep sigh before she said in a more practical tone, "I pleaded and begged him to believe me! I swore on the Bible and on my mother's head that I was telling him the truth."

She looked at him and then continued, "I said it was Sadira in whom you were interested, Sadira you were courting. You stayed telling me how much in love with her you were until the early hours of the morning."

"And he believed you?" the Earl asked sarcastically.

"He *wants* to believe me," Daphne replied, "but he will only permit himself to believe that I am unblemished and still faithful to him if you will do what I have said you will. That is to call this morning to ask permission to marry his daughter."

"And if I refuse?" the Earl asked.

"Then, because Arthur is so obstinate, I know he will start divorce proceedings immediately, as he threatened to do, last night."

She rose from the sofa and walked across the room to put her hand on the Earl's arm.

"Please, please, I beg of you, save us both," she pleaded. "I love you, and it would be Heaven to be with you always, but you know as well as I do that the humiliation and misery would kill us."

Her fingers tightened on his arm as she said, "How can I be . . . sneered at and . . . spurned by the women who have . . . been my friends?"

The Earl did not reply and she went on, "How can I be deprived of my position as Lady-of-the-Bedchamber to Her Majesty the Queen?"

She gave a little sob before she added, "How could we . . . go abroad to live in some sleazy French town? We should hate it there . . . because of what we were missing in England."

The Earl knew this was true, and he was well aware that that was what a divorce would entail. He was thinking too of how much it would hurt his family, for if the Marquess was proud, so were the Kensalls.

Every Earl had played his part in the history of

England. There had of course been some spendthrifts, some incompetant Statesmen, and some extremely tiresome characters. But there had never yet been a social scandal in the family. At least, certainly not to the point where the reigning Earl had been taken through the Divorce Courts.

Nor for that matter, had a Kensall been executed in the Tower of London.

To suffer the latter, the Earl thought, might indeed be preferable to facing life with Daphne in exile away from everything that he possessed and enjoyed.

There was silence until Daphne said, "I must go. I only managed to get here by pretending I wished to attend a Service in Grosvenor Chapel."

"Alone?" the Earl queried.

"No, of course not. My maid came with me, but she is a fervent Methodist and disapproved of what she looks on as Popish ritual. So she sits on a chair at the entrance and will not enter the Chapel itself."

She looked at the Earl to see if he was listening.

"I slipped out by a side-door, and as I will return by the same route my maid will not be aware that I have visited you."

"I sincerely hope not!" the Earl exclaimed. "If that information were passed on to the Marquess it would make things even worse than they are already."

Daphne wiped her tears from her eyes.

"Only *you* can save us both," she said. "I am sure Arthur will be at home all the morning, but do not leave it too long or he may go to the Solicitors. Then he will refuse to see you and it will be too late."

The Earl felt as if he was dreaming and this could not be true.

"And what about your Stepdaughter?" he managed to ask. "Supposing she knows that I have been with you and tells her father she has never even met me?"

"You can leave that to me." Daphne assured him. "All you have to do is to convince Arthur that you wish to marry his daughter."

As she spoke Daphne glanced at the clock on the mantelpiece.

"I must go!" she exclaimed. "You had better let me out through the garden-entrance into the Mews. It would be quicker than going out by the front-door."

The Earl did not argue. He merely opened the French window as Daphne pulled her veil back over her face.

Without speaking they walked quickly down the garden to where there was a door behind a clump of rhododendrons. The Earl opened it.

As he did so Daphne looked up at him. "I am so sorry, Norwin, that this has happened," she said, "but we have to save ourselves, and this is the only way."

She did not wait for an answer but slipped away.

The Earl could hear her footsteps as she ran down the cobbled surface of the Mews. It was only a short distance to the Grosvenor Chapel, and he thought that with any luck the Service would not be over before she got there.

As he shut the garden-door and returned to his study he wondered if he had imagined what he had just heard. It could not be true! This could not really be happening to him! But it had happened, and he was committed because there was no other way out.

He had to ask the Marquess for his daughter's hand in marriage. Yet he did not even know what the girl looked like.

It was either that, or what to him would be condemnation to an intolerable existence.

Then as he looked up at the sky, he said fervently as so many other men had before him, "How in the Devil's name did I get myself into this mess!"

CHAPTER TWO

The Marchioness of Langbourne slipped into the Grosvenor Chapel and found that the Service was just over. The congregation was moving towards the West Door. She joined them and saw her Lady's-maid waiting in the porch.

Without speaking she started walking as quickly as she could to Langbourne House in Park Street. As she went in through the front door the hands on the Grandfather clock pointed to nine o'clock.

She had given orders before she went out that His Lordship was tired after his journey home from France, and he was therefore not to be called until nine o'clock with his breakfast.

She ran up the stairs and went to her Stepdaughter's bedroom at the end of the corridor. She entered without knocking.

Sadira was standing at the window dressed in her riding-habit. She turned round as her Stepmother entered and asked, "Why was I told not to leave the room until you had spoken to me? I hear Papa is back, and I want to see him."

"Your father was very tired last night," the Marchioness replied, "and he has only just been called."

"Then can I go to him now?" Sadira asked.

"Not until I have spoken to you," the Marchioness insisted.

She had shut the door behind her when she entered. Now she walked across the room to stand in the window near Sadira. There was silence.

Then as Sadira looked questioningly at her Stepmother the Marchioness said, "Later this morning the Earl of Kensall will be calling on your father to ask if you and he can announce your engagement."

Sadira looked at her Stepmother in sheer astonishment. "What are you . . . saying?" she asked. "Whatever are you . . . talking . . . about?"

"I am telling you," the Marchioness replied, "that you are to marry the Earl of Kensall."

Sadira drew in her breath.

"I will do nothing of the sort! I am not a fool, Step-Mama! I know quite well that he has been seeing you almost every night that Papa has been away."

"You may know that," the Marchioness said coldly, "but you will not repeat it to your father. In fact you will tell him that you are delighted by the Earl's attentions and thrilled to be his wife."

"I think you must be crazy!" Sadira expostulated. "I have no wish to marry the Earl – in fact I would not marry him under any circumstances!"

There was a pause between the words.

She was trying to speak without being offensively rude to her Stepmother.

The Marchioness walked to an armchair and sat down. "Now listen to me," she said. "Your father reviled me last night because he had me watched while he was away."

Sadira pressed her lips together as if she would say something, but with an effort she remained silent.

'I told him," the Marchioness went on, "that he is entirely mistaken in what he assumed and that the Earl had come here to see you."

"That is a lie!" Sadira said, "And I do not believe Papa could be so stupid as to believe it."

"I think I have convinced your father that he is mistaken, and you therefore have to bail me out. When the Earl invites you to be his wife you must accept with pleasure."

"Of course I will not!" Sadira fumed. "Do you really think, Step-Mama, that I would be willing to marry a man who is infatuated with you?"

She paused a moment to glare at the Marchioness.

"If you want the truth, I am shocked at the way you have behaved in my father's absence."

"Whether you are shocked or not," the Marchioness retorted, "you will do as I say. Otherwise there will be an enormous scandal which will affect you as well as me and distress the whole family."

"If there is a scandal, it is your doing," Sadira replied, "and I can only say that my mother would never have behaved in the way that you have!"

The Marchioness leaned back in the chair. "Are you saying," she said slowly, "that you will not support my explanation of what has happened and will refuse to marry the Earl of Kensall?"

"I will tell Papa the truth," Sadira said defiantly. "Whatever action he decides to take in this matter will be between you and him and has nothing to do with me!"

The Marchioness's eyes narrowed. "Very well," she said, "if that is your attitude, then I shall make you suffer as I will suffer!"

The way she spoke made Sadira look at her nervously.

"What are you . . . saying?" she asked.

"I remember your telling me when we were last in the country," the Marchioness said, "that you loved your horse *Swallow* and your dog *Bracken* more than anything else in the world."

"What have they to do with it?" Sadira asked quickly.

"If you will not help me," the Marchioness replied "I will have *Swallow* taken to a place where you cannot find him and he will be given nothing to eat and nothing to drink until he dies."

Sadira gave a cry of horror and her Stepmother went on, "I will take *Bracken* to the slums somewhere in the East End and give him to one of those hardened criminals who beat their dogs when they have had too much to drink."

"I . . . do not believe you!" Sadira cried. "Nobody could be so cruel . . . so wicked as to treat . . . animals in such a way!"

"You can of course save them," the Marchioness said coldly. "Otherwise I promise you I shall do what I say, and they will suffer as I shall suffer if your father divorces me."

Sadira started.

"Papa intends to . . . divorce you?" she questioned.

"That is what he will do," the Marchioness replied, "unless you convince him that he is wrong in his assumptions and that you are delighted to make such a brilliant social marriage."

Her voice altered as she said furiously, "Do not be such a fool, girl! Every young woman in London has attempted to catch the Earl of Kensall! But he has remained a bachelor despite every effort that has been made to trap him into matrimony."

"And now you think you have succeeded," Sadira said sarcastically.

"The Earl has accepted the situation and will call on your father some time this morning. If you are going riding, you will return in no more than an hour and having changed will be waiting for him."

Sadira turned towards the window as if she could not bear to look at her Stepmother. Then she said in a small voice which was very different from the way she had spoken before, "Do I . . . have to do . . . this?"

"There is no alternative," the Marchioness said. "And make no mistake, if you are not convincing and your father does not believe you, then you will never see *Swallow* or *Bracken* again!"

She paused for breath before she went on, "And do not think you will get away scot-free. If you ruin my life. I will ruin yours. There will be at least a little while before it becomes known what your father is doing."

She looked at Sadira to see if she was listening.

"In the meantime I shall make it my business to inform every hostess in London what you are really like."

"What . . . I am really . . . like? Sadira exclaimed in surprise.

"I will tell them," the Marchioness said dropping her voice, "that your immoral behaviour has upset and distressed your father. That you have had clandestine affairs with the grooms who accompany you out riding, and that I have had to dismiss two footmen because you made advances to them."

Sadira gave a cry of sheer horror and the Marchioness continued:

"You know as well as I do how such a story would circulate like a wild wind amongst the gossips of Mayfair."

She paused a moment and then went on harshly, "You may deny it, you may try to live it down, but it will be repeated and repeated until, like your animals, you are in the grave!"

She almost spat the words at Sadira.

There was silence as Sadira looked out of the window with unseeing eyes.

The Marchioness rose to her feet.

"I am not making idle threats," she said. "My future life depends entirely on you, just as your horse and dog do if they are to live."

There was no reply from Sadira.

Knowing she had won the battle, the Marchioness went from the room. In her own bedroom she powdered her face until she looked very pale. Then she deliberately drew a dark line under her eyes where none had been naturally.

She then changed from the dark gown she had worn to go to Church into one that was frilly and feminine. It took her sometime, and when she looked at the clock she knew that the Marquess would now be dressing himself.

She went to his room.

When she knocked on the door it was opened by his Valet.

The Marchioness passed the man without speaking, and he tactfully went into the corridor closing the door behind him. Inside the room the Marchioness stood with her back to the door.

Her husband was dressed with the exception of his coat.

He was brushing back the sides of his hair as he stood in front of the mirror. The hair was going white and there was a bald patch on the back of his head.

He did not turn round and when the Marchioness did not speak he asked in a hard voice, "What do you want?"

"I . . . came," the Marchioness replied in a soft, childlike voice, "to see if . . . you are still . . . angry with . . . m, me."

"What do you expect?" her husband replied.

"I . . . I have been crying all night . . . because you did not . . . believe me."

"I am not a fool," the Marquess said, "and I have the evidence here to show me exactly how you behaved after I left to go to France."

"That is what . . . you said . . . last night," the Marchioness replied, "but I told you the truth . . . only you . . . refuse to believe me."

"As I said I am not a fool," the Marquess answered.

The Marchioness came a little nearer to him.

"Please, Arthur," she said, "please . . . talk to Sadira and of course to the Earl of Kensall before you accuse me . . . in this . . . way."

The Marquess put down his hair-brushes.

"Where is Sadira?" he asked. "Why has she not come to see me?"

"She wanted to do so, but was told you were asleep and so went riding," the Marchioness said. "But she will be back in a short time and then you will know that I am telling . . . you the . . . truth."

She gave a little sob that was very effective.

"I love . . . you . . . I have always . . . loved you! How can you think I would look at any other man . . . except . . . you?"

Her voice broke on the last words.

As if she could control her tears no longer she ran from the room, leaving the door open behind her so that the Marquess could hear her running down the corridor.

He sighed and picked up the Detective's report, which was lying on the top of the chest-of-drawers. Putting it into his pocket he walked slowly and heavily down the stairs to his study.

There was a large amount of paperwork waiting for him on his desk, but although he sat down he did not touch any of it. Instead he stared ahead with the eyes of a man who has received a body blow and finds it hard to bear the agony of it.

The Earl of Kensall arrived at Langbourne House at eleven o'clock.

It was only a short distance from his own house in Park Lane, yet because it was a formal occasion he travelled in one of his carriages. He was also dressed formally, telling himself mockingly that he might be making a friendly call on the Marquess rather than going to his execution.

He could imagine nothing more appalling than being forced into matrimony with a girl he had hardly seen, who would doubtless be aware that he was the lover of her Stepmother.

If she was not aware of it, then she must be half-witted, and indeed he suspected most débutantes were. He would therefore doubtless find her incredibly boring for the rest of his life.

As his horses swept him down the street he tried to think of any possible way out of this appalling situation. He could however, find no alternative.

Even to think of the horror of being subjected to Divorce proceedings made him shudder, and he could imagine how appalled his relatives would be. His enemies would laugh and say he had received his "just deserts". For those who had always been jealous of him would be able to crow loudly.

To live abroad would be, he knew, a hell on earth. How could he leave his estates, his race-horses, his hunters and his friends?

He reached Langbourne House, and looked at the pillared front door he had entered surreptitiously so many times in the past weeks.

As he did so, he knew he hated Daphne Langbourne. She had enticed him into the ignominious position in which he now found himself. Yet there was only one possible way by which he could extricate himself, and that was if he could lie convincingly enough to deceive the Marquess.

The humiliation of it all was appalling.

He wanted to tell his footman who had jumped down to the pavement that he had changed his mind. His carriage would drive on. But then he would have no other resource and the Marquess would go ahead with the divorce as he had threatened. Though it might take many months, during which the gossips would talk of nothing else, the end was inevitable.

He would be exiled from everything that mattered to him.

His footman rang the bell. The door was opened immediately which told the Earl that he was expected. Feeling that every step took him nearer to the guillotine, he descended from his carriage and walked into the hall.

"Good morning, M'Lord!" the Butler said respectfully.

With an effort the Earl forced himself to reply.

Without being asked whom he wished to see, so that the Earl knew that Daphne had given her orders, he was led down the corridor to the study.

He knew the room well.

Daphne had always waited for him in the Drawing-Room which was a perfect frame for her beauty.

Or else in her bedroom.

She had given him a key so that he could let himself into the house without, she thought, the servants being aware of it.

Now the Earl thought rather belatedly that it would have been wiser if she had let him in, perhaps through the garden at the back of the house. The detective who had watched him had obviously seen him enter and leave by the front-door, while everybody else in the house was supposedly asleep.

The Butler opened the door of the Study. As he did so, the Earl thought there was so much evidence against him that nothing he could say would make the Marquess believe anything but what was the truth.

As he entered the Marquess rose from behind his desk. At a quick glance the Earl thought he looked aggressive. He had also aged considerably since he had last seen him only a few weeks ago, and there were lines on his face that had not been there previously. He could not help being aware that the older man was suffering.

Only the Earl's strong self-control and the fact that he was fighting virtually for his life made him appear at ease.

In what appeared to be a friendly, normal tone of voice he said:

"Good morning, My Lord! It is nice to see you back in London again, and I feel sure your mission to Paris has been as successful as the Prime Minister hoped."

The Marquess moved from his desk to stand in front of the fireplace.

"I understand you wanted to see me, Kensall," he said harshly.

"Yes, indeed," the Earl replied. "I have come to ask you for your permission to marry – Sadira."

There was a distinct pause before he said the last word.

And for one rather terrifying moment the Earl had forgotten her name.

The Marquess looked at him sharply. "This, surely, is somewhat unexpected?" he remarked.

"Not really," the Earl replied. "I fell in love with Sadira as soon as I saw her, and we have been seeing each other every day while you have been in France."

He forced a somewhat crooked smile to his lips before he added, "I think we will be very happy together as we both have a passion for horses which is a deep bond in common."

The Marquess moved from where he had been standing in front of the fireplace, and went slowly across the room to the window. With his back to the Earl he said as if he was thinking out every word, "Sadira is very young. It seems strange, in view of your reputation, that you should be interested in a girl who knows nothing of the social world in which you move."

"I can understand your feeling that," the Earl replied, "but surely you realise, my Lord, that what a man looks for in a wife is very different from what he finds enjoyable as a bachelor?"

There was silence.

The Marquess turned from the window.

"Is what you are saying to me the truth, Kensall?" he enquired. "Are you really in love with Sadira, and will you make her the sort of husband I want for my daughter's happiness?"

The Earl raised his eye-brows, as if he was surprised.

"I cannot imagine, my Lord, why you should suspect I am telling you anything but the truth," he answered, "or why you should question my desire to make your daughter my wife."

He thought as he spoke that he was being clever in taking the initiative. It was better than continuing in a somewhat defensive role, but he knew the Marquess was fighting a desire to accuse him outright of having seduced his wife. He was therefore determined that, if it was possible, such words would not be spoken, as they would open up a chasm into which Daphne and he would fall.

"What I am asking," he said briskly, "is that you allow us to announce our engagement and plan our wedding for later in the year."

He paused for a moment and then continued, "I realise that Sadira is very young, and I would not want to deprive her of attending the many Balls which take place in the Season."

He gave a short laugh and said "She is entitled to them, although I must say they bore me. But we want to be together, and of course that is easy while we are both in London."

Again there was an uncomfortable silence which made the Earl feel apprehensive.

With an obvious effort the Marquess said slowly, "I will talk to Sadira, and if her wishes are the same as yours, then of course I must agree."

"Thank you, my Lord! Thank you very much indeed!" the Earl said with an air of affected gaiety. He had been afraid ever since he had entered the room that the Marquess would express what was uppermost in his mind.

"Now that you have given me your permission," the Earl said, "perhaps I could see Sadira and tell her the good news?"

The Marquess walked over to his desk and, picking up a gold bell, rang it.

The door was opened immediately and as the Butler appeared he said, "Send Lady Sadira to me."

"Very good, M'Lord."

The two men were alone again and the Earl said conversationally, "I hope to have a winner tomorrow at Kempton Park. Will you be attending the meeting?"

"I do not know," the Marquess said in a tired voice. "I had not expected to be in London for another week."

The Earl knew this was dangerous ground. He might be told the reason why the Marquess had hurried home.

"Well, if you do go," he said quickly, "I suggest you put a small amount on *Triumph*, which I am running in the second race, and there is a chance I shall be successful in the fourth with a horse called *Lightning*."

The Marquess did not reply and the Earl went on, speaking rapidly, "This will be the first time he had been tried out in a big race. I have great faith in him, and I would value your opinion after you have seen him run."

The Marquess had moved back to his desk. He was looking down at something that lay in front of him on his blotter. The Earl suspected it was the detective's report covering Daphne's movements while he had been away, and, that it was this which had brought him hurrying home from France.

The Marquess did not pick up the paper, he merely

stared at it. As he did so the door opened and Sadira came in.

As he looked at her the Earl was astonished. He had, in fact, no idea what she would look like. He had suspected that, if she took after her father, she would be tall, heavily-built and perhaps passably good-looking, but not at all outstanding.

Instead he saw a slim, sylph-like figure. With his long experience of women, as he glanced at her face he knew she was different in every way from any woman he had seen before.

There was no doubt that she was beautiful, yet there was nothing conventional about her looks. Her hair was fair, but of a colour that resembled the rays of the sun, when it first rose over the horizon. Her skin had the translucence of a pearl, and her eyes were blue, but not the conventional blue of an English Beauty. They were the blue of the Madonna's robe and as brilliant as the Mediterranean Sea. Very large, they seemed in fact to dominate her small, pointed face, and there was a sensitivity about her which surprised the Earl.

He knew it was something he had never seen before, and as their eyes met he was aware without her having to say so that she both hated and despised him.

Sadira looked away from him towards her father. Then she ran to the desk and put her arms round the Marquess's neck. "You are back, Papa!" she exclaimed. "I have missed you so much! Did you enjoy yourself in Paris?"

The words seemed to come quite spontaneously to her lips.

The Earl however was aware that she was acting her part as well as he had acted his.

"I came back," the Marquess replied slowly, "for reasons we need not discuss. I understand from the Earl of Kensall that he wishes to make you his wife. Do you wish to marry him?"

Sadira forced a smile to her lips.

"Has he told you the news, Papa? I do hope you are pleased."

Listening, the Earl thought she had avoided the question rather cleverly.

"I suppose," the Marquess said, "if that is what you want, I must give you my blessing and hope you will be very happy together."

There was an unmistakable note of doubt in the last words, but Sadira ignored it.

She merely kissed her father again saying, "Dearest Papa, there is a great deal to plan and to talk about, but if you will allow us to become engaged, there is no need yet to worry about the wedding."

The Marquess rose from his chair. "I assume," he said, "that you wish to celebrate the decision you have made, so I will go and order something that is appropriate with which to drink your health." He did not sound at all elated about it, and went from the room closing the door somewhat sharply behind him.

Sadira stood very still as if she was turned to stone and looked at the Earl.

"I must commend you," he said, "on playing your part very skilfully."

"As I imagine you played yours!" she retorted.

"There was nothing else we could do," the Earl said grimly.

"Nothing," Sadira agreed.

She was thinking as she spoke of how her Stepmother had threatened to destroy her horse and her dog. She wondered if she had thought up anything so effective but cruel herself, or whether the idea had come from the Earl.

She was not yet a part of the social world. But she was well aware that for somebody in her Stepmother's position to go through the Divorce Courts was to sink into the gutter.

Sadira had been very young at the time but she could remember the endless gossip there had been. The Prince of Wales had been cited as a co-respondent in the Mordaunt case. For weeks nobody had talked of anything else. Their voices had seemed to grow louder and louder as every tit-bit of information was relayed. Then it was repeated a thousand times until the newspapers could produce something even more sensational.

The Prince of Wales had defended himself.

He had come out of the case officially without a stain on his character, but nobody wanted to believe that was the truth.

Sadira could remember her Governess saying to the Housekeeper. "He's got away with it, but who is going to believe it?"

She knew that her father must not be involved in a divorce-case which would be equally notorious. It would strike at his pride and the dignity for which she had always admired him. But she supposed the same could be said of the Earl, for she was well aware that he was spoken of as the most handsome and attractive bachelor in society, as well as being the most wealthy.

Because she was interested in horses, she had followed his career on the racecourse and she knew how many winners he had in his stable.

She was also sure that her Stepmother was wildly and passionately in love with him for the Marchioness could not contain her excitement when she was able to see him without her husband being aware of it.

Sadira was too astute not to know that there had been other men also in her Stepmother's life, but she had never attached much importance to them. In fact, she was prepared to ignore them as long as they did not interfere with her father's happiness.

He did not see the irrepressible radiance in his wife's face when she knew he was going away for a few days. He might miss it because he was getting old, but Sadira noticed, and hated her Stepmother and despised her for her infidelity.

When she thought of how she had taken her mother's place she wanted to cry. Yet because she was very intelligent she understood that her father needed a woman at his side, and she had to admit too that her Stepmother had made her father happy. Because she was so beautiful, he was proud of her.

Now Sadira thought of herself being married to a man who loved another woman, and that woman her own Stepmother. It was a humiliation which made her feel as if she would never be able to hold up her head again.

She walked from behind the desk to stand a little

nearer to the Earl, as she was afraid that anyone outside in the corridor might hear what they said. It was certainly not because she wanted to be close to him.

"I suppose," she said in a low voice, "it is possible for us to remain engaged for some months, and then I could refuse to marry you at the last moment?"

The Earl did not answer at once.

At last he said:

"We could of course try that, but I rather fancy that your father, having accepted me as his son-in-law, will insist on our marriage, if only to convince himself that the unpleasant report he has does not tell the true story."

Sadira knew exactly what he was saying. She thought in a way he was more astute than she had expected.

She knew that her father would find it difficult if not impossible, to forget altogether what had made him return to England so precipitately, and he would therefore be watching them. Any attempt to terminate their engagement would undoubtedly arouse his suspicions. He might even then seek to divorce his wife and cite the Earl as co-respondent.

It all passed through her mind. As it did so, she knew that the Earl was thinking the same thing.

"What can we . . . do?" she asked.

"Nothing," the Earl answered.

"But . . . there must be . . . some way . . . out?"

He shook his head.

"I doubt it. The detective's evidence would be very convincing, and even now I am quite certain your father is suspicious that we are not as interested in each other as we are pretending to be."

Sadira put her hands up to her face. The words that came to her lips were, she knew, so offensive that she dared not say them. Instead she sat down at her father's desk.

Without consciously doing so she unfolded the piece of paper which lay on top of the blotter. Only as she looked at it did she realise what it was.

It was in the form of a Diary. There were notes against each day as to what time the Earl had entered the house after dark and what time he left. She looked at it with an expression of disgust and he realised what she was reading.

He walked quickly to the desk and picked up the piece of paper. One glance at it told him that his suspicions were correct.

"There is no reason for you to read that." he said angrily, "and the sooner it is forgotten, the better."

"You may be able to forget it." Sadira said coldly, "but I assure you it is something I shall never forget – nor will I ever forgive you!"

"It would be better to try," the Earl suggested. "Otherwise we have no chance of even attempting, to make the best of a bad job."

"You can try," Sadira said, "but I hate and despise you for hurting my father, and of course for spoiling any chance I have of happiness in the future."

It flashed through the Earl's mind that most young women would be perfectly content to marry him, whatever his reputation. He found it hard to believe that this beautiful girl should be so antagonistic.

She looked like a piece of Dresden china or as if she had stepped down out of a picture by Botticelli.

Men of his age were expected to have had numerous love-affairs before they led their bride down the aisle, but if she had any inkling of what her bridegroom had done in the past she chose to forget it.

It was easy to do so in the delight of having an unassailable position in Society. And in the case of somebody like himself, of having a great deal of money to spend and magnificent houses in which to live.

But Sadira was looking at him with her unusual blue eyes. He had the uncomfortable feeling that she was telling the truth and she would neither forget nor forgive.

"Now listen to me," he said. "We are both aware that this is a very unfortunate situation in which to find ourselves."

He paused a moment, before continuing, "But if we are sensible, we can start by being friends. I am sure we will find we have a great number of interests in common – horses, for one."

Sadira did not answer, and he went on, "You are very young and therefore, like most young women, you see everything in black or white. What we all have to do in life is to accept that there is good and bad in everyone, and it is very much more comfortable to ignore the bad."

"You are very plausible, my Lord," Sadira answered, "and I will certainly consider what you have said. At the same time, I find it difficult to make excuses for the Devil!"

She spoke softly but clearly, and the Earl could not think of an answer.

Then, before he tried to do so, the door opened. The Marquess returned followed by the Butler carrying a silver tray on which there was a bottle of champagne.

CHAPTER THREE

The Earl put down his empty glass.

"I have an appointment," he said, "so I must now leave you. But I will return this afternoon with an engagement ring which I am sure Sadira will cherish, as my mother cherished it when she received it from my father."

He hoped as he spoke that he sounded like a man in love.

Now for the first time there was a faint smile on the Marquess's lips. "If you are coming back, Kensall," he said, "then I suggest you come to dinner."

What that meant flashed through the Earl's and Sadira's mind at the same moment, for nothing could be more uncomfortable than to dine with the Marchioness.

Only the very quick thinking enabled the Earl to reply, "It is most kind of you, My Lord, but I am sure you will understand that it is very important that my grandmother should meet Sadira and hear the good news before any other members of the family. I would like to take Sadira to dine with her this evening."

"In that case," the Marquess agreed, "I must withdraw my invitation." He was beginning to look more cheerful.

The Earl thought he was at least three-quarters of the way to being convinced that what they had told him was the truth.

"I will come to see you tomorrow," he went on, "but if you have time this afternoon, please put the announcement of our engagement in the *London Gazette* and *The Times*."

He stopped speaking to look at the Marquess. "I will notify all the important members of the Kensall family during the afternoon," he concluded.

"I will do as you suggest," the Marquess replied, "and of course, my daughter can help me."

The Earl turned to Sadira. "Goodbye until this evening," he said, "and I will call for you at about seven o'clock."

"That will be lovely!" Sadira managed to reply with what sounded like a genuine enthusiasm in her voice.

The Marquess was watching them and as the Earl moved to the door, he said to his daughter, "You had better see your young man out as I suspect he wants to have a last word alone with you."

"Of course, papa," Sadira replied.

She went out of the Study with the Earl, closing the door behind them. "That was clever of you," she said in a low voice.

"I really do want you to meet my grandmother." he

replied, "and I will send a note to her immediately telling her that we will be with her at seven-thirty. You will understand that she dines early."

"Of course," Sadira answered.

They had reached the hall by now where the Butler was waiting.

"I have to hurry," the Earl said. "It is always a mistake to keep the Prime Minister waiting."

"Yes, but tell your coachman to drive carefully," Sadira admonished.

"I will do that," the Earl replied.

He hurried out through the front door.

As Sadira went upstairs she thought they had now convinced everyone, including the servants, of their relationship. Then as she went to her own room she asked desperately how she could do this.

How was it possible for her to marry a man whom she hated and despised? A man who she knew had no wish to marry her.

"What ... can I ... do? What can I ... do?" she murmured.

Because she did not want to encounter her Step-mother, she stayed in her bedroom until luncheon-time. Then when she heard the gong being sounded she reluctantly went downstairs.

Her father and Stepmother were just coming from the study. "Oh there you are, Sadira!" the Marquess said. "I was just relating the good news to your Stepmother and of course she is delighted!"

Sadira thought there was a touch of sarcasm in his voice, but before she could speak the Marchioness said gushingly, "Oh, dearest Sadira! What wonderful news! I am so happy for you, and I cannot think of anyone who would grace the position of the Countess of Kensall better than yourself!"

"Thank you," Sadira replied. "I thought you would be pleased, and I know I am very, very lucky!"

She tried to speak as if she was a young girl swept off her feet by her first love-affair.

They went into luncheon. The Marchioness talked of the trousseau Sadira would need and that the sooner they started shopping, the better.

Sadira knew that her father was listening. At the same time, her instinct told her he still half-suspected that he was being deceived. She therefore put out her hand to touch his. "Stepmama is going too fast," she said. "While I am thrilled and delighted to be engaged to Norwin, I do not wish to leave home too soon. You know, Papa, I am always happy when I am with you."

The Marquess's eyes softened.

"And I like having you with me," he said, "but I must accept that will be impossible now you are preoccupied, as you will be, with your fiancé."

"I still want to be with you every moment that you can spare for me," Sadira replied.

Somehow they got through the meal.

Sadira felt as if she was walking a tight-rope and at any moment she might slip and fall. She had no idea what she ate, but she noticed that when her Stepmother was not being over-gushing she was looking at her with a hard look in her eyes.

"She hates me as much as I hate her!" Sadira thought. "How could Papa have married such a woman?"

She thought the only consolation in having to marry the Earl would be to get away from the Marchioness's evil presence, for she felt as though the whole house was poisoned by it.

After luncheon the Marchioness suggested that she might like to go shopping. Sadira replied however that she had some letters to write.

"I suppose you want to tell your friends that you have beaten them to the Matrimonial Post?" her father said in an effort at being humorous.

"You are quite right, Papa," Sadira replied, "and I know they will all want to be bridesmaids."

"I am sure they will," he agreed, "and they will be grinding their teeth all the way up the aisle!"

Sadira managed to laugh, but at the same time she could not help thinking that was what she herself would be doing. Her father had however put an idea into her head.

She decided she would go to see her closest and dearest friend Anne Beecham. They had known each other since childhood, and had shared a Governess for several years and had then gone to the same finishing school. Anne was very much more intelligent than most of their contemporaries, and had therefore, at school, shared with Sadira the extra tutors whom the Marquess ordered for her.

Feeling that she must talk to someone, Sadira knew that the only person she could trust would be Anne. They were so close to each other and often said they were like sisters. Sadira knew nothing she told Anne would be passed on to anybody else.

At the same time, she was nervous of hearing Anne's reactions to anything as unpleasant and sordid as the position she was in at the moment. Although she had known of her Stepmother's infidelity she had never told Anne about it. She had tried to pretend even to herself that it was not happening, and because she loved her father she had only prayed he would never know.

He would be intolerably humiliated by it.

Now she had been forced to save the Earl and her father from being involved in a Divorce Case. She wondered if it was really to her father's advantage to live for the rest of his life with a woman who was nothing more than what people called "a common whore".

"I cannot think clearly while I am in the same house with her!" Sadira told herself, and rang the bell for her maid.

When she came Sadira told her to order a carriage and she was to accompany her. "I am visiting a friend," she confessed.

Unlike the Marquess, Anne's parents, Lord and Lady Beecham, spent most of their time in London, only going to the country when they stayed with friends.

Because Anne, like Sadira, loved riding she had enjoyed staying at Langbourne Hall where she rode the Marquess's horses and did everything else that Sadira enjoyed.

They had planned how often they could be together during the Season when they were both debutantes. Lord Beecham was giving a Ball for Anne and the Marquess was giving one for Sadira. They were both to be presented at the first Drawing-Room, and as they would be invited to the same Balls, their parents could take it in turns to give dinner parties for them.

"I must see Anne,' Sadira thought, "only she will understand."

A short while later Sadira was driving towards Anne's house, turning over in her mind exactly what she should say.

"I will tell her the truth," she decided, "and Anne will understand."

At the same time she shuddered from actually putting into words the horror she felt at her Stepmother's behaviour. She also shrank from explaining the degrading position she had to accept in order to deceive her father as she knew that Anne woud be as shocked at the whole situation as she was herself.

The carriage drew up outside Lady Beecham's house in Belgrave Square, and only then did Sadira think that perhaps it would be a mistake to tell Anne the whole truth.

It would be better just to say that her father and Stepmother had arranged her marriage without consulting her. But of course she was pleased at having such an important Bridegroom!

When the front door opened she realised she was not the first visitor. In the hall were men's top-hats and a number of sunshades, which told her that Lady Beecham was entertaining.

"Good afternoon, M'Lady," the Butler said who of course knew her well.

"Good afternoon, Watkins," Sadira replied. "What is happening today?"

" 'Er Ladyship's got a meeting, M'Lady, of one of 'er charities to 'elp the heathens."

Sadira's spirits sank. She knew only too well that Anne's mother was a very religious woman, who spent a great deal of her time and money in helping charitable causes. Indeed on one occasion Sadira had been dragged in to make what were known as "Mother Hubbards". These were, she recalled, very ugly dresses for one of the African countries, where the children were naked and their mothers in very much the same condition.

When Sadira stayed with Anne she had to be down early for breakfast because family prayers always took place in the Dining-Room before Breakfast was brought in. All the staff attended, and either Lord or Lady Beecham presided. They read the Collect of the Day followed by a number of prayers to which the congregation were expected to reply with fervent "Amens".

Now as Sadira seemed indecisive, the Butler said, "If I were you, M'Lady, I'd slip into th' back of th' room, and when Miss Anne sees you she'll come away as quick as possible."

"That is a good idea," Sadira smiled.

The Butler led the way to the Dining-Room.

Sadira knew that now it would be filled with chairs, which would face towards a table at the end of the room at which Lady Beecham and the organisers of the Charity would be seated.

There would not be a large audience, if it was anything like the meetings she had attended before. Those who were there would all be middle-aged or elderly friends who came because Lady Beecham asked them to; and because they knew that after the meeting was over there would be an excellent tea which would take place in the Drawing-Room.

Sadira thought that when the audience moved she and Anne could slip upstairs. They could talk in what had once been the School Room but was now her friend's Sitting Room.

Watkins opened the door quietly. Sadira slipped past him into a vacant chair that was right at the back. As she did so she was aware that a man was giving a lecture, and was not surprised to find that it was about North Africa, a part of the world in which Lady Beecham was particularly interested.

Sadira had learned quite a lot in the past about Africa from the various Charities Lady Beecham supported. Now she noticed that the man speaking had white hair and a kind face, and spoke in a deep, positive voice.

He was describing a Camel Market and making it easy to imagine the men with their great beasts. He told them of the women sitting on the sand and selling home-made goods or twirling wool into yarn on hand-spinners. "They use," he said, "big skeins of coarse stuff, while the baby camels nuzzle against their mothers."

He then went on to describe how hard the women worked, and how difficult it was for a number of them to feed their children and keep alive.

To her surprise, Sadira found herself deeply interested in what he was saying. This Speaker certainly knew his subject, and he also spoke with an unmistakable sincerity.

Having heard so many of them, Sadira had learnt to tell which Speakers were genuinely concerned with the

Charity for which they were raising funds. Others merely repeated what they had read or had been told to say.

The man with white hair went on to speak of the lack of medical help. It led, he said, to a great deal of unnecessary suffering, especially amongst the women. "It is not only a question of medical supplies," he went on, "but the knowledge of those who administer them is very limited, and many children die because there is no one who can tell their mothers how to treat them."

He paused to look round his audience before he continued, "The women themselves frequently have an agonising time in childbirth."

He told his listeners how the countries of North Africa were still entirely a man's world. The women had their faces covered and waited on their husbands at meals, where they were allowed to eat what was left after their husbands had finished.

Another need, he said, was schools for the children. Technicians also were desperately lacking in everything that concerned the economic development of the region.

"I am," he said with a faint smile, "just a voice crying in the wilderness. To send out Medical Missionaries like myself costs money, and that is not available unless people like yourselves are warm-hearted enough to help us, not only with your prayers, but also from your purses."

He sat down and there was rather more applause than usual on such an occasion.

Lady Beecham, who had been listening intently, rose to her feet.

"I know you will want me to thank Father Christopher," she said, "for his wonderful address and for all we have learned about the women of North Africa. I need not ask you to give generously because I know you will do so."

She paused and then continued, "Father Christopher will be leaving England in two days time, and I am sure we want to send him back with enough money to help at least some of the women and children who are suffering."

She was about to say something more when Father Christopher, who had sat down, rose again.

"I think we should make it clear, my Lady, so that there is no mistake," he said, "that while I spoke of North Africa in general this afternoon, I am in fact, when I leave England, going first to Morocco."

He paused and then said, "I am told I am urgently needed in what to the Muslims is the Sacred City of Fez, and I know that all I have said this afternoon applies especially to that country."

He sat down again and Lady Beecham said, "You know, Father, that we wish to help you wherever you go. Your wonderful work has already been commented on by Her Majesty the Queen, and we know that any money we give you will be spent in the best possible way."

Father Christopher nodded as if in agreement and Lady Beecham then added, "I hope now that you will all come to the Drawing-Room for tea, and of course to talk to Father Christopher personally. Any donations you feel able to give us will be collected at the door."

Those who were seated at the table rose to be followed by those in the audience. As they did so they all started talking so that the room seemed to vibrate to the sound of it.

Anne, who had seen Sadira come in, joined her. "Let us escape while we can!" she whispered.

They slipped out through the door before anybody else had reached it. Running through the Hall they hurried up the stairs to Anne's Sitting-Room.

As they reached it Anne exclaimed, "I am so glad to see you, Sadira! What has been happening? Have you been asked to any parties yet? I have had three invitations!"

Sadira drew in her breath before she said, "I have something to tell you, Anne dear."

"What is it?" her friend asked.

"Papa has arranged that I am to . . . marry . . . the Earl of . . . Kensall."

Anne stared at her in astonishment.

"Marry – the Earl of Kensall?" she repeated after a moment. "But I had no idea you even knew him!"

"I know him now," Sadira said, "and my engagement is being announced to-morrow."

"I do not believe it!" Anne exclaimed. "How can it all have happened so quickly? You never said a word to me about it when we met the day before yesterday."

"I did not . . . know it . . . myself then," Sadira replied.

"And he has asked you to marry him?" Anne said as if she was working it out for herself. "But, surely, this has all happened too quickly? How can you know if you really are in love with him?"

They had often said to each other that they would never marry until they were really in love. Sadira knew that was what Anne was referring to, and before she could think of a reply Anne added, "I suppose, because your father is so grand, that you are being treated like

Royalty and are having an arranged marriage! Oh,
Sadira, we always said we would never agree to a
marriage like that!"

"I . . . know," Sadira answered. "But Papa thinks that
the Earl of Kensall . . is . . different from . . . other men."

"Which of course he is!" Anne remarked. "I have heard
about him because everybody says how handsome he is.
Once Papa made some remark about his love-affairs, but
Mama said 'Hush!' and put her fingers up to her lips
because I was present."

She had said all this before she put her hand up as if to
stop herself.

"Oh, darling," she exclaimed, "I am sorry. I should not
have said that to you! But it is such a surprise! I thought
we were going to spend at least half the Season together
before either of us got engaged."

"I . . . know," Sadira answered, "but it is something I . . .
cannot do . . anything about. I just wanted you to . . .
know about it before it . . . appeared in *The Gazette*."

Anne rose and kissed her friend.

"I love you, Sadira," she said, "and you know that the
one thing I want is for you to be happy. If you are, that is
all that matters."

Sadira wanted to say that she was miserably unhappy
and that was why she had called to see her. But she knew
it would be a mistake to say any such thing. There was
nothing Anne could do except commiserate with her.

She suddenly decided that she did not want to talk
about it any more. The whole idea of it was too appalling
to discuss. If they talked and talked as women always did,
it would only make everyting worse.

Impulsively she said, "I will tell you what I would like, Anne. I would like to meet Father Christopher. I was very interested in what he was saying. Perhaps after that we could come up here again and I can tell you about my engagement."

"Of course, if that is what you want, dearest," Anne agreed, "and naturally I want to hear everything about your . . . future."

She hesitated over the words.

Sadira was aware, because they knew each other so well, that Anne suspected there was something wrong, but was, however, too tactful to say so.

She only took Sadira by the hand and they went slowly down the stairs they had just run up so quickly.

Lady Beecham's large and attractive Drawing Room was full of the people who had attended the meeting.

There was a delicious tea laid out at one end of the room and a number of maids and footmen to serve it, who carried round every sort of sandwich, scone, biscuit and cake. The Beechams were known for their outstanding hospitality.

Sadira knew that most of those present at Lady Beecham's invitation to support good works came because of the food rather than the cause.

Lady Beecham was a rather stout woman who had once been pretty like her daughter, and she greeted Sadira with affection. "How sweet of you, dear child, to come and help me," she said. "We have had one of the best meetings I can ever remember."

"I would like to meet Father Christopher," Sadira said.

"Of course," Lady Beecham replied.

She took Sadira by the hand and drew her towards
Father Christopher. He was talking to several ladies who
appeared to be paying him gushing compliments.

Lady Beecham swept them to one side. "I want you to
meet, Father," she said, "my daughter's greatest friend,
Lady Sadira Bourne, whose father is the Marquess of
Langbourne. She was just telling me how interested she
was in your talk."

The Father held out his hand. "I like to think," he said,
"that I am not too prosy for the young."

Sadira laughed. "Of course not! I thought you painted
in words a very eloquent picture of what is happening in
a country I have longed to visit."

The Missionary smiled at her. "Then it is something
you must do when you have the opportunity."

"I have always wanted to go to Morocco," Sadira went
on. "Have you been there before?"

"Several years ago," Father Christopher replied, "and
they have asked me particularly to visit them again. There
are, I believe, a number of Christians in the City of Fez
who are feeling neglected."

"Then I am sure they will be delighted to see you,"
Sadira replied, "especially as you are a Medical
Missionary."

She remembered hearing that Medical Missionaries
were far more respected than those who simply tried to
wean the natives from one religion to another. The
difficulty was to find enough men prepared to spend
four years on medical training. They thought it
unnecessary when all they wanted was to preach the
Gospel.

"Are you going alone, or are other Missionaries going with you? Sadira asked.

"On this occasion I am going alone," Father Christpher replied, "but I always hope that I shall have a disciple who will allow me to teach him in practice, rather than learning it in a Classroom."

Sadira smiled. "I can understand that," she said, "and I should have thought there were hundreds of students who would prefer to be 'in the fray', so to speak, rather than just swotting it up in books."

Father Christopher laughed. "That describes it very eloquently. But you would be surprised how difficult it is to get young men to accept training during what they think of as 'the best years of their lives' rather than riding into battle."

Anne, who was standing beside Sadira, laughed at this. "I rather sympathise with them," she said. "But if I were a man I would come with you, Father Christopher!"

"And I am sure you would be a very great help. But you would find the ship in which I am travelling to Tangier very uncomfortable."

Father Christopher paused and with his eyes twinkling said, "Instead you must help me by getting your friends, like Lady Sadira, to remember that while they curtsy to Her Majesty in Buckingham Palace, there are those in the world outside who are often very hungry."

"I will do that," Anne said simply, "and I know Sadira will help me."

"You have an Arab name, Lady Sadira," Father Christopher said. "It means 'From the Water'!"

"I did not know its meaning," Sadira said, "but my

father chose it because he loves to travel and enjoyed Africa when he visited it."

"Then I feel I am quite justified in asking you to remember that land," Father Christopher said, "and especially the people I shall be tending in Morocco."

"I will do that," Sadira promised. "Anne and I will force our friends to be generous, even when they do not want to be."

Father Christopher shook his head. "What is given willingly is more acceptable to God."

Some other people came up to speak to him and Anne said to Sadira, "I am sure we can collect some of the money he requires."

"I will ask Papa for a donation to-night," Sadira replied. "As you know, he is always very generous."

"So is my father, if I get him in the right mood," Anne said. "Do you want to talk to anybody else?"

"No, not really," Sadira answered, "and I think after all I should now go home. Papa only arrived back from France yesterday and I have hardly seen him."

She knew this was an excuse that Anne would understand, for she was well aware of how Sadira loved being with her father.

"Come and see me tomorrow," Anne pleaded. "I want to show you my new gown in which I am to be presented. It is absolutely beautiful and Mama spent a fortune on it!"

"I have not yet had a chance to go shopping," Sadira replied.

"Whatever you wear you will look simply marvellous!" Anne said enthusiastically.

"I might say the same to you," Sadira retorted.

Anne was very pretty, but her looks did not compare in any way with the unusual beauty of her friend. Aloud she said, "If I am told that anyone at Buckingham Palace looks lovelier than you, Sadira, I shall not believe it!"

"You may be quite certain that we will not eclipse any of the sophisticated Beauties," Sadira replied. "They will make us appear very 'small fry'!"

She found herself thinking that the one person who would really try to outshine her would be her Stepmother.

Driving back in the carriage after leaving Anne, Sadira felt depressed.

She knew that the Marchioness would try to eclipse her not only at Buckingham Palace, but she would do so every day in every way when they were at home. Sadira was not so foolish as not to know that while it was for her Stepmother's benefit that she was saving the Earl from the Divorce Courts, the Marchioness was fiercely resenting her. This was because Sadira was marrying the man whom she herself loved.

"She hates me," Sadira reasoned, "as she always has. And now, as I am taking her place in becoming the Earl's wife, she will want to kill me!"

She could understand in a way the agony the Marchioness would suffer when she bore the Earl's name. She would be consumed with jealousy when they went away on their honeymoon and when she sat at the opposite end of his table. What was more, it was a hatred, Sadira thought, which would be echoed by the Earl himself.

If he loved her Stepmother as he obviously did, he too would suffer. Especially when he was forced to introduce her as his wife, and when he had to behave politely towards her in the presence of other people, or when he saw her wearing the Kensall diamonds as his mother had. Even when she received his guests in his different houses.

Hatred, hatred, hatred!

She could feel it vibrating all around her. She thought it would be impossible to live in a world where there was no love, no friendship.

"I cannot bear it . . . I cannot live . . . like that!" Sadira told herself.

The carriage reached the house in Park Street. As she went in through the front door her Stepmother came out from her father's Study, and looked at Sadira with suspicion in her eyes before she asked, "Where have you been? You did not tell me you were going out!"

Sadira did not answer.

The Marchioness reached out and grabbing her by the arm dragged her into the nearest room. She shut the door, then said, "How dare you leave this house without telling me where you were going! If you have been to visit Norwin, I can tell you here and now that he has no wish to have you running after him! The best thing you can do is to keep out of his way."

Sadira stared at the Marchioness in astonishment. It had never entered her mind that her Stepmother would think that she was running after the Earl. Now she could see the fury in her eyes and the contortion of her lips!

As she spoke so scathingly and offensively, Sadira saw she was consumed with jealousy. In a cold voice she replied, "I have not been to see the Earl of Kensall. And if I had, I hardly think you are the right person to reproach me for doing your dirty work for you!"

With a cry of fury her Stepmother reached out and slapped Sadira viciously across the face. "How dare you speak to me like that!" she raged. "You are lucky, very lucky to be able to marry such a man. At the same time, do not forget that it is me he loves – me – not you!"

As if her fury made it impossible for her to say any more, the Marchioness turned and went out of the room. She slammed the door behind her so violently that the china ornaments rattled.

Sadira stood very still.

She could feel the sting of her Stepmother's hand on her cheek, but she did not touch it. She only told herself that this was something she could not and would not endure.

CHAPTER FOUR

The Earl called to take Sadira out to dinner and, surprisingly, he was late. When he arrived he did not get out of the carriage, but told the footman to inform Her Ladyship that he was sorry he had been delayed, and asked that she would come as quickly as she could.

Sadira was already waiting and she hurried into the Hall. The Butler put her velvet wrap over her shoulders. Only as she got into the carriage beside the Earl did she realise that he was being very clever.

He obviously had no wish to see her Stepmother. By coming for her ten minutes late he had the perfect excuse to say that they must hurry away immediately.

He put out his hand to take hers as she sat down beside him. "I apologise," he said, "and I know you will understand that my grandmother is a very punctual person."

"Just like my mother," Sadira answered.

They drove off. The Earl was silent until they had nearly reached his grandmother's house which was in Wilton Crescent. Then he said, "My grandmother was very kind to me when I was a boy, and I know that you will convince her that we are going to be happy. It would make her miserable if she thought I was not."

"I understand," Sadira answered coldly.

She thought as she spoke how infuriating it was to have to act a part with everybody she met. Then as the candlelight in the carriage illuminated her hair and her face the Earl asked unexpectedly, "What have you done to your cheek?"

For a moment she did not know what he meant. Then when she saw him looking at where the Marchioness had struck her she felt her own anger rise at the memory of it.

She was tempted to retort, "It is the way the woman you love treats me." Then she thought that would be a vulgar thing to say and her father would disapprove of it.

Instead she replied, "I do not . . . wish to . . . speak about . . . it."

She looked away from the Earl as she spoke, and therefore did not realise that an understanding look had come into his eyes. His lips had tightened as if he was preventing himself from saying something he might regret.

Then the Butler was standing in the doorway and the footman opened the door of the carriage. Sadira stepped out. As she went into the Hall there was the scent of bees-wax and lavender, which reminded her of how Langbourne Hall used to smell before her Stepmother took over.

She had swept away the homemade bowls of pot-pourri and lavender, which were replaced by exotic French perfumes which permeated the whole house.

"Her Ladyship's in the Drawing-Room, M'Lord," the Butler said respectfully. He led the way and opened a door.

Sadira saw at once that the room was furnished exactly as she had expected. Again it reminded her of her home before her Stepmother had changed everything, with a comfortable sofa and arm-chairs round the fireplace. There were flowers everywhere which she was certain had not been bought in London, but brought up from the country.

The Dowager Countess was seated in an armchair with a pretty lace antimacassar behind her head. A Chinese embroidered shawl covered her knees. As the Earl advanced towards her she held out both hands in delight.

"Norwin, I am so thrilled to see you!" she exclaimed. "We were all so excited when I received your message saying you were dining here."

The Earl bent to kiss his grandmother.

Sadira could see that she had once been very beautiful. Her appearance was still striking with her dead white hair and an elegance which was ageless. She had several ropes of perfect pearls round her neck, and she was also wearing diamond earrings with pearl drops at the ends.

"I am delighted to see you, Grandmama," the Earl said, "and this is a very special occasion because I have brought Sadira Bourne with me."

"I wondered who would accompany you," his grand-mother replied.

She held out her hand to Sadira and as she did so the Earl said, "Sadira has promised to be my wife, and I know, Grandmama, you would want to be the first to hear of it."

The Dowager Countess gave a little cry. "Your wife!" she exclaimed. "Oh, Norwin, how wonderful! As you must have guessed, it is something I have been waiting to hear for a very long time."

She was holding Sadira's hand and did not let it go. She looked at her scrutinisingly and said, "You are very lovely, my dear, and very like your mother who was a friend of mine."

"You remember Mama?" Sadira asked.

"Very well indeed," the Dowager Countess replied, "and I can imagine nothing more perfect than that you should marry my grandson."

She looked up at the Earl and asked, "Why did you not warn me? I had no idea that after all these years you were contemplating becoming a married man!"

"I did not contemplate it at all," the Earl said with a smile, "until I met Sadira."

"And she is everything you ever wanted," the Dowager Countess said quietly.

Because she was obviously so delighted at the news Sadira felt uncomfortably guilty at deceiving her. There was however nothing she could do, but hope she would never discover the truth.

The Butler announced dinner and the Dowager Countess took her grandson's arm. He led her into the Dining Room while Sadira followed behind them.

The meal was what she expected, plain food beautifully cooked, and Sadira was not surprised to hear that the

Cook had been with the Dowager Countess for nearly thirty years.

She thought the same might also be true of the Butler, and also of the Housekeeper whom she had encountered when she went up stairs after dinner to tidy herself.

It had been an unexpectedly interesting meal. The Earl had exerted himself to tell his grandmother many things she wanted to know about what was happening on his Estate in the country.

There was also a great deal of conversation about his horses; a subject about which the Dowager Countess had a surprising knowledge.

Sadira found herself listening intently and enjoying the Earl's jokes.

After dinner the Dowager and Sadira returned to the Drawing-Room and left the Earl to his port. Now that they were alone the Dowager Countess said, "I have never been so happy as I am to-night. I know, my dear, that you are exactly the wife I wanted Norwin to have."

"I hope I will . . . make him . . . happy," Sadira said a little uncomfortably.

"Of course you will," the Dowager answered, "and you will help him to forget how unhappy he was as a child."

Sadira must have looked surprised for the Dowager Countess explained, "Norwin was only eleven when his mother died and I have never known a boy to be so unhappy. I did my best, as did our other relatives. But we had to leave him to be brought up by his father, with whom he never got on, and he was miserable."

"Why should that have happened?" Sadira asked.

"I suppose my son, who was rather a strange character, was in a way jealous of Norwin."

The Dowager Countess paused, then added, "I think a man can often be jealous of his own son because he will eventually take his place, and also if his son is brilliant in sport as he himself had always wanted to be."

"It seems rather strange," Sadira murmured.

"I agree," the Dowager Countess replied. "Yet it does happen, and without his mother Norwin had a very difficult time with his father always finding fault with him and stopping him from doing anything he wanted to do."

The Dowager gave a deep sigh before she went on. "This continued until, when he grew up, Norwin seldom went to Kensall Park, which we all regretted."

She put her hand on Sadira's arm as she said, "I know, my dear, that you will try to make up for all he suffered as a boy, and take him away from the fast, heartless people who run after him because he is rich and important, but never attempt to understand him."

Sadira looked down. She felt she could not meet the old lady's eyes. Hers might reveal that she also did not understand the Earl, nor did she wish to.

"Now everything will be changed," the Dowager Countess went on as if she was speaking to herself, "and Norwin will have somebody who loves him for himself rather than for his possessions."

Sadira knew that the Dowager Countess was thinking of the women like her Stepmother who had pursued him. Like the Marchioness, they would fight to keep the Earl's love even when he was married to her.

She could hardly tell his grandmother that she did not care what he did, nor with whom he spent his time, as long as it was not with her. She only felt that the future was going to be more complicated than she had expected.

She wished she did not have to pretend to this dear old lady that she loved her grandson. She must never guess that it was impossible for her to make up for his unhappy childhood.

"I must not feel sorry for him," she told herself.

It was then the Earl came into the room.

"I have been to the kitchen, Grandmama," he said, "to tell Mrs. Field the good news. She is absolutely delighted and is determined to make my wedding-cake. But you know as well as I do that it will infuriate my own Chef!"

His grandmother laughed. "Then you will just have to have a wedding-cake in every house you own," she said, "and two in London!"

Her eyes softened as she said, "It is like you, Norwin, to tell Mrs. Field. I know she must be thrilled. She has been in a tizzy ever since you sent the message saying you were going to dine here."

"We will dine with you again next week," the Earl promised, "and then Sadira can meet all the old servants, as she will have to do in the country, and of course at Kensall House."

"The tenants and the whole village," the Dowager said, "will expect a special feast on your Wedding Day."

"They shall have fireworks and barrels of ale," the Earl promised.

He looked at the clock and said, "I know it is nearly

your bedtime, Grandmama, so I am now going to take Sadira home."

"I think the truth is," his grandmother answered softly, "that you want to be alone. Take me up to bed, and you can stay here comfortably in front of the fire."

She gave a little laugh before she added, "I remember, years ago, when your grandfather was courting me, it was very difficult for us to get a moment alone to ourselves. There were always people round us, so sometimes we used to slip away from them and hide in the garden."

"Surely, in your day, that was vastly improper," the Earl teased.

"Of course it was!" his grandmother answered, "Once we found a hiding-place in the attic and I got into terrible trouble with my mother."

Her eyes twinkled as she added, "But it was worth every moment of it!"

The Earl offered her his arm. "Let me take you upstairs, Grandmama," he suggested.

"You can take me to the foot of them" the Dowager retorted. "My lady's-maid will be waiting there. You remember she is Lucy, who used to be your nursery-maid."

"Of course I have not forgotten Lucy," the Earl answered.

He escorted his grandmother from the rom, and before she left the Dowager Countess kissed Sadira affectionately on both cheeks.

"You have made me very happy, dear child," she said. "One day, when you can spare the time, come and see me and I will tell how naughty and at the same time how adorable Norwin was when he was a little boy."

"I do not mind your doing that," the Earl said, "but leave Sadira to find out for herself how much I have 'blotted my copybook' since then!"

He spoke jokingly, but as Sadira met his eyes she had the feeling that he was challenging her in some way.

When he and his grandmother had left the room she stood looking down into the fire. She felt that if only this charade they were acting were real, how differently she would be feeling now. She had always wanted to marry a man who had a knowledge of horses, who was athletic, and whose home was in the country.

It was one of the dreams she had shared with Anne.

Now the background was right, but everything else was wrong. The Earl was in love with a woman he could not marry. She knew that every moment they were together he was wishing it was her Stepmother who was beside him.

As she thought of the Marchioness she put her hand to her cheek which was still burning. "How can I possibly . . endure this sort of thing . . . happening to me . . . not only now, but in the future?" she asked.

She could envisage the years ahead as the Marchioness encroached more and more upon them. Eventually she herself would become nothing but a pale ghost moving about the great house in which she was not wanted, unnoticed and alone.

When the Earl came back into the room Sadira did not turn round.

He walked towards her and when he reached her he

said, "I can only say thank you for making my grand-mother so happy."

"I dislike having to lie to anybody who is so kind and who loves you so much," Sadira said in a low voice.

"I feel exactly the same," the Earl replied.

Sadira thought he was going to say something more. Instead he said abruptly, "Let me take you home, unless there is anywhere else you would rather go?"

"I would like to go home," Sadira answered quietly, but she knew as she spoke that that was untrue, for the Marchioness might be waiting for her. If she could choose, she would rather be anywhere than under the same roof with her Stepmother.

The carriage was waiting and they drove back in silence. Only as they neared Langbourne House did the Earl say, "My grandmother suggested, and I think it is a good idea, that tomorrow we have luncheon with my Aunt, Lady Winterton. She will invite a number of cousins and other relatives whom you will have to meet sooner or later."

Sadira did not speak and he went on, "Our engagement will be announced in the newspapers to-morrow, and it would be a mistake to give them cause to ask why they had not been notified before its appearance."

He looked at her before he went on "We can, in this way, prevent there being any complaints by meeting them before you go to any other parties."

"I understand," Sadira said. "At what time will you call for me?"

"At half-past twelve," the Earl replied, "and I feel sure

your father will understand if he is not invited to this luncheon."

Sadira knew what he was implying.

It was that his Aunt would not want her Stepmother to be included in the invitation.

"I am sure Papa already has an engagement for to-morrow," Sadira said quickly.

The carriage arrived at Langbourne House, and the Earl got out to help her alight. They went into the hall and because the servants were listening the Earl said, "Good-night, Sadira, and thank you again for what has been a very happy evening."

To her surprise he then took her hand and raised it to his lips. She knew he was once again play-acting, but at the same time, she had to admit that he played his part very gracefully.

As he left the house she said to the Butler, "I would like you to know that His Lordship and I are engaged to be married. The announcement will be in the newspapers tomorrow morning."

She saw the astonishment in the Butler's eyes before he said quickly, "That's very good news, very good news indeed, M'Lady, an' of course I wish you and His Lordship every happiness."

"Thank you," Sadira replied.

She ran up to her bedroom, but did not ring for her maid. Instead she undressed herself, and when she had put on her nightgown she pulled back the curtains.

It was a clear night, with the stars shining over the garden at the back of the house and turning the distant roofs to silver.

"What shall I . . . do?" Sadira asked them.

"How can I go on with this . . . farce?"

As she spoke she felt as if her Stepmother was there, menacing her, and preparing to strike her again.

"It is impossible . . . quite impossible," she murmured.

Then suddenly, as if the stars were telling her, she had an idea. It seemed impossible, and yet she knew it was a way out. It was going to be difficult, very difficult, yet because the stars told her what she would do, she knew it was possible.

Just possible, if she was clever enough.

"Thank you . . . thank you," she said in her heart.

She closed the curtains and got into bed, not to sleep, but to think and plan.

The next morning Sadira went riding early. She stayed in the Park so long that when she finally returned to the house it was to learn that her Stepmother had gone out.

She changed her clothes, putting on one of her prettiest gowns and a most attractive hat.

The Earl called for her punctually at half-after twelve. Sadira knew he did not wish to come into the house, and she was therefore waiting for him in the hall. As soon as the carriage drove up she was on the doorstep, and there was therefore no reason for the Earl to alight.

To-day he had brought an open carriage and they drove off in the sunshine, with the coachman and footman on the box looking very smart. The two horses which drew them were perfectly matched and extremely well-bred.

It was easy to talk about them and the Earl's other horses and to avoid the subject of themselves.

His Aunt's house was a large one. Despite herself, Sadira found the Kensalls were all charming and delightful people, who were obviously thrilled that the Earl was to be married.

They went out of their way to let Sadira know how pleased they were that she was to be his bride.

Of course, they never mentioned her Stepmother.

She knew instinctively, however, they were thinking that she had been a bad influence on the Earl, and they disliked his name being linked with hers in gossip; although they would have been far too frightened to say so to him.

So it was with genuine delight that they welcomed Sadira into the family.

"What a pity this is not true," she found herself thinking, not once but dozens of times during the visit especially since every one of the Earl's relations wished to entertain her.

When at last they left, the Earl had half-a-dozen dates written down on a small pad which he carried in his pocket.

They got into the carriage and as they did so Sadira said, "Would it be possible on the way home to call for a few minutes at 29 Belgrave Square? There is something I particularly want to ask my friend Anne Beecham."

"Yes, of course," the Earl agreed.

He told the footman that was where they were to go first and they moved off into the sunshine.

"You were a huge success," the Earl said. "Every one of my relations acclaimed you as if you were an Angel sent from Heaven!"

"They were . . . very kind," Sadira answered, "and I hate deceiving them . . . as I hated doing last night to your grandmother."

"Fortunately," the Earl replied, "they will never know that they have been deceived, and they will therefore be your devoted admirers and, I hope, your friends for the rest of your life."

Sadira did not answer and he said, "There are a number of my other relatives I want you to meet, but they live in the country, and I think we should spend a few days at Kensall Park as soon as it can be arranged."

Sadira thought this was another thing that would infuriate her Stepmother.

The Earl must have known what she was thinking, for he said quickly, "I thought perhaps, as your father is so busy, I could ask one of my Aunts to chaperon you so that there would be no need for him to leave London."

"That is a good idea," Sadira managed to reply.

They reached 29 Belgrave Square and she said a little hesitatingly, "I do not suppose . . . you want to . . . come in and so . . . as I shall only be a minute or two . . . it might be easier for you to . . . stay in the carriage."

"That is what I will do," the Earl replied.

Sadira alighted. The door of the house was opened by Watkins.

"Good afternoon, M'Lady," he said.

"Good afternoon, Watkins. Is Miss Anne in?" Sadira asked.

"She's upstairs in her sitting room, M'Lady. I'spects you can find your own way."

"Yes, of course, Watkins," Sadira answered, "and is your rheumatism any better?"

The Butler shook his head.

She knew that was the reason why he had no wish to climb the stairs unless he had to, so she ran up the stairs quickly and burst in on Anne who was writing at a desk by the window.

She jumped up with excitement. "Sadira!" she cried. "I had no idea you were coming to see me."

"I have only dropped in on my way home," Sadira answered, "I want to tell you that I think I have some money for Father Christopher."

"How splendid!" Anne said. "I have not yet had a chance to ask Papa, and I expect he will resent having to give money to me as well as Mama."

"Then you must try some of the people who have not yet already been approached," Sadira said. "But tell me when is Father Christopher leaving? I thought he said tomorrow."

"That is right," Anne replied, "and some of the people who were at Mama's meeting are going to see him off."

"Where is he leaving from?" Sadira enquired.

"From Tilbury, and his cargo-boat, which is called *Idris*, is sailing at ten o'clock. I know this because I have just had to tell one of Mama's friends who is taking him some money, quite a lot, I believe."

"How splendid to have collected it so quickly," Sadira said, "and if I get what I expect from Papa I will see that he has it before he leaves."

"You are making me feel as if I have been very lazy,"

Anne said, "but I have really not had much time. I am writing out invitations now for Mama's next Charity, which is for people who are suffering after an earthquake in Turkey."

"Your mother is wonderful!" Sadira said. "She is always helping somebody who is in dire need."

"I know," Anne replied, "but *I* have to write the invitations!"

Sadira kissed her friend. "I would help you, but I must not keep the Earl waiting. He is in the carriage outside."

"I will peep at him out of the window," Anne said. "I saw the announcement of your engagement in the newspaper to-day, and I do wish you every happiness, Sadira! I am going to save up to give you a wonderful wedding-present."

"Thank you, thank you!" Sadira answered. "Now I must go. I told the Earl I would be only a minute."

Watkins bowed her out and she waved to him as they drove away.

"I suppose your friend, Anne, will be one of your bridesmaids?" the Earl remarked.

"She will be my chief bridesmaid," Sadira replied. "We have known each other since we were very small and she is my best friend."

"Those are the friends who matter," the Earl said. "One knows that whatever trouble one is in they will always stand by and never let one down."

Sadira thought that in the sophisticated social set in which the Earl moved there would be few people on whom he could rely if he was in real trouble.

Real trouble – for instance being co-respondent in a Divorce Case with her Stepmother!

They reached Langbourne House. As the carriage came to a standstill Sadira held out her hand. "Thank you very much," she said to the Earl, "I enjoyed the luncheon and I think your relatives are all charming, and also very fond of you."

"That is what I think myself," the Earl answered, "and I am grateful to you for being so pleasant to them."

He did not take her hand, but got out of the carriage first in order to help her to the ground.

Sadira wondered if perhaps he wished to come into the house, but he said quickly, "I doubt if your father is at home and I have a great deal of work to do. Perhaps you will give him my regards and say that I shall expect to see him at dinner tonight."

"Tonight?" Sadira questioned.

"There is a special dinner being given by the Secretary of State for Foreign Affairs," the Earl explained, "and I know your father will be one of the guests."

"Yes," Sadira replied, "they are great friends."

"I suppose," the Earl asked reflectively as if he had just thought of it, "I could ask if I could bring you, now that we are officially engaged."

"No, no, please," Sadira objected. "I have a great deal to do, and actually I think I have had enough excitement for one day."

"Then we will meet tomorrow," the Earl said. "I am sure there will be a family luncheon of some sort, and I will let you know as soon as it is arranged."

"Thank you," Sadira said, "and – good-bye!"

She walked into the house and the Earl got back into the carriage.

As he drove away he thought that for someone so young and inexperienced Sadira had come through a very difficult ordeal with flying colours. He could not imagine anyone else he knew who could have carried it off first at the intimate dinner with his grandmother and then at the luncheon today. Sadira had not made a single mistake.

He was sure there was no suspicion in anybody's mind that things were not as they appeared. As he looked back, he realised that everything Sadira had said and done was exactly right. Everyone in his family whom she had met so far were hysterical with delight about her.

He was thinking as he drove home that once again his luck had not failed him.

Inside the house, Sadira found with relief that both her father and her Stepmother were out. She went up to her bedroom and locked the door.

She then went into the wardrobe room which adjoined it, and picked up two large canvas bags, which were what she had used at School.

She had needed them when the girls were taken on expeditions involving a stay for one or two nights at the places they visited. Because the girls invariably had to carry their own luggage, they used canvas bags which were lighter than leather cases would have been.

Now Sadira took from her wardrobe the plainest and simplest clothes she possessed and packed them neatly. She knew it would be a mistake to be carrying anything surplus to essentials.

She therefore discarded a great many gowns, keeping strictly to what was necessary, and when the two bags were packed she replaced them in the wardrobe room, locked the door and took away the key.

By this time it was growing late in the afternoon. But she knew that, if her father was at the House of Lords, he would not return until a little later.

Sadira went to his bedroom, where her father had a special safe to which, apart from him, only she knew the combination. It was when her mother was ill and rather weak that she had been told how to open it, to enable her to put away her mother's jewellery, for this was something that the maids were not allowed to see or do.

Sadira locked the outer door to her father's bedroom so that his Valet could not come in and interrupt her.

She opened the safe and, as she expected, she found a considerable amount of money in it. There was also some small change, as he never left it lying about in drawers. She went through the bank-notes and took for herself what seemed to her to be a very large sum, but at the same time she knew she would need it all.

She also took some sovereigns and half-sovereigns, knowing that she herself possessed very little ready money.

Her father had always said that she could have what she wanted, but he thought it a mistake for her to carry much money on her person. She therefore gave all her bills to his Secretary. Now, Sadira knew, she had to look after herself.

She had to be practical and work out as near as she could what she would need to last her for a long time.

Finally, when she had taken almost everything her father had in the safe, she locked it. Then she went back to her own bedroom.

When her maid came in she was writing letters at her *secretaire* which stood in a corner of the room near the window. She brought in a bath that Sadira would take before she dressed for dinner.

Having finished what she was writing, Sadira put the letters into envelopes and hid them underneath the blotter. She remembered that her father and Stepmother would be going out to the same dinner as the Earl, and she would be alone. She thought she would have her meal brought up on a tray.

"I am tired," she said to the maid, "and I shall go to bed early, but now I am going to walk for a little while in the garden and get a breath of fresh air."

"It's cooler now th' sun's gone down, M'Lady," the maid replied, "an' I'll have your bath ready for you when you comes back."

"Thank you," Sadira replied.

She went downstairs, not hurrying, and out through the French windows into the garden. It was narrow, as were the gardens of the houses on either side of it, but it went back quite a long way to the Mews.

This was where her father and the owners of the neighbouring houses kept their horses and carriages.

She went out through the door at the end of the garden leaving the lock on the latch.

As her father and Stepmother were going out to dinner the coachman and the footman would be on the carriage. There would therefore be no-one with the other horses in the stable.

The doors to it were shut to as Sadira walked down the Mews.

There was a groom whose Master was a very old man. Her father knew him well, but he had been ill for some time. His groom was usually to be found sitting outside his stabledoors, or, having little to do, talking to other grooms.

When Sadira visited her father's horses, which she did frequently, he was often there and always greeted her politely. She usually asked him how his Master was and he would reply grimly, "'Is Lordship ain't no better, and me an' 'is 'orses don't get enough exercise, but there ain't nothin' Oi can do 'bout it."

Sadira felt rather sorry for him.

Now she walked a little way down the Mews where he was usually to be found. To her relief she saw him through the open door of the stable where he was rubbing down one of the carriage-horses and whistling as he did so.

"Good-afternoon, Britan," she said.

"A'ternoon, M'Lady," he replied. "Oi sees in th' newspaper as ye be goin' to be married, an' Oi 'opes ye'll be very 'appy."

"Thank you," Sadira replied.

"An' wot a man ye've chosen! 'Is 'orses be some o' th' best. Oi allus 'as a bet on 'em wen Oi 'as a chance."

"Well, I only hope they will not disappoint you," Sadira replied.

There was silence for a moment. Then she asked, "I wonder if you would do me a service?"

"Oi'll do wot Oi can," Britan answered. "Wot be ye askin' me, M'Lady?"

"I want to go very early tomorrow morning to Tilbury docks," Sadira replied, "but I am anxious that no one in my house should know what I am doing. Can I trust you to take me there and say nothing about it to anybody?"

"Cross me 'eart an' 'ope t'die!" Britan declared. "Wen Oi gives me word, Oi keeps it!"

"That is what I hoped you would say," Sadira said. "I will tell you what I want you to do."

Britan stopped grooming the horse and came to stand beside her. "Wot's Yer Ladyship up to?" he asked. "A bit o' romance?"

"Perhaps that is what you would think it is," Sadira said, "but as I told you, no one must know."

"Oi've given me word," he replied.

"Then could you please be waiting here for me at six o'clock tomorrow morning?" Sadira asked.

Britan nodded and she said, "I have two bags which I want to take with me. If I take them into the garden while the staff are having their supper, perhaps you could collect them without anybody being aware of it."

"Trust me, M'Lady."

"I will put them just inside the garden door," Sadira said. "Here is the key."

She put it into his hand.

As he took it he looked up and asked, "Noo, M'Lady, wot be ye up to? Ye're not elopin', be ye, 'cause if ye are, ye'll break 'is Lordship's 'eart."

"No, I am not doing that," Sadira said. "I need to go away for a short time, but I have been forbidden to do so. That is why I want your help."

She thought he looked indecisive and she added, "I know I can trust you."

"'Course ye can."

"If you know nothing and say nothing, then you cannot be held responsible for anything that happens to me," Sadira said, "so, please . . . please, once you have dropped me at Tilbury, forget about it."

"Oi'll not do that," Britan answered, "but Oi won't say nothin'."

"I will certainly make it worth your while," Sadira said with a smile and adding, "Six o'clock, or perhaps I had better say a quarter to six, or our coachman might be up."

"Don't ye fret," Britan said, "that lot don't strain 'emselves, unless they 'as to."

"Very well, then," Sadira said. "I will be with you at six o'clock sharp."

"Oi'll be waitin'," Britan promised, "an' yer bags'll be inside t'carriage wi' ye."

"Thank you, and I am very grateful," Sadira replied.

She hurried back into the house, having left the garden door locked behind her.

She had a bath and put on a negligée. The meal that was brought up was delicious, but Sadira was too excited to be hungry.

She was embarking on an adventure. It was not only the most outrageous thing she had ever done, but was also the most dangerous. Yet the stars had shown her the way.

She knew that somehow they would help and protect her.

When she was left alone she took her bags downstairs at a moment when she knew the servants would be having their supper. The senior servants ate in the Housekeeper's Room and the others in the Servants' Hall. None of their windows faced onto the garden.

Wearing her nightgown and negligée she went out through a French window onto the lawn. It was growing dusk, and she was sure that no one would notice her as she carried first one of the canvas bags, then the other.

She set them down beside the garden door to which Britan had the key. Then she went back into the house. In her room she took from beneath the blotter the two letters she had written.

One was to her father and one to the Earl. To the latter she attached with a clip a piece of paper on which she had written a note, "*Please have this taken during the morning to the Earl of Kensall.*"

She went downstairs and put the envelope addressed to her father on his desk. She knew he always went to his study after breakfast, and her Stepmother would still not have been called as she was seldom woken before ten o'clock.

Sadira went back to her bedroom. "I have thought of everything!" she told herself.

Then as if she was compelled to do so she went to the window and pulled back the curtain. By now it was nearly dark. The first stars were beginning to twinkle in the sky. She looked up at them. "Show me the way," she said. "I know you will not fail me."

Everything was very quiet.

She had the feeling that there was a sudden peace

within herself, and the fear and the horror had subsided.

"The stars will protect me," Sadira whispered, "I know they will."

She got into bed and fell asleep almost at once.

CHAPTER FIVE

The Earl awoke early and felt in need of some exercise. He thought that only on horseback would he shake off the depression from which he had been suffering for the last two days. So he went to the stables himself, and five minutes later he was riding towards Rotten Row, mounted on a stallion he had bought only a week before at Tattersall's Sale Rooms.

He was delighted to find it was very obstreperous. It reared and bucked to show its independence, and it took the Earl some time to get it under control. There was nothing he enjoyed more than the age-old battle between man and beast, and when finally the stallion settled down to a steady trot he knew he was the victor.

It was too early in the morning for there to be any of the beautiful women who drove in their carriages down Rotten Row. They invariably waved to him expecting him to stop and talk to them, but he hoped however that he might see Sadira.

He knew she rode early, but to-day there was no sight of her. He was thinking of how tactful and charming she had been yesterday with all his relatives, so that in consequence he was not so apprehensive about the future as he had been.

When he arrived back at Kensall House he would have gone straight into the Breakfast Room. Before he could do so however, he was told by the Butler there was a note for him from Langbourne House.

This information swept the smile from the Earl's face. There was a frown between his eyes as he went to the sideboard to choose what he would have for breakfast.

He was certain that the letter in question came from the Marchioness, and he thought it both indiscreet and very tiresome that she should write to him at the moment. He had already received one passionate letter which he read quickly before he threw it into the fire. This second one would share the same fate.

"It is always the same," he told himself angrily, "a woman will never give up and wants a brief *affaire de coeur* to last for ever!"

It was dangerous for her to write anything which the Marquess might see. And also very stupid. The knowledge of what was waiting for him was spoiling his breakfast, but he refused to hurry.

He deliberately read both *The Times* and the *Morning Post* before finally he walked towards his study. His Secretary had arranged the usual pile of invitations, besides which there was another pile of private letters.

On his blotter was the letter which he knew was from Langbourne House.

He glanced at it and was at once aware that it was not addressed in the Marchioness's handwriting. That, he thought, showed a little more sense. Nor had she used her private writing-paper which was heavily scented.

Yet it made him angry that she should have written again. Therefore he put the note to one side and went through the invitations. He marked those he accepted with a tick and those he rejected with a cross. Then he read his other personal letters which his Secretary did not open.

Now he looked once again at the note from Langbourne House. He sighed and opened it. As he unfolded the piece of paper inside the envelope he realised it was not from the Marchioness, but from Sadira.

Wondering why she had written to him he read:

My Lord,

I have been thinking over our situation and I realise that if I am suffering, so are you, only in your case it is worse.

I am aware that when we are together you are wishing that someone else was beside you, and I think it would be impossible for us to go through life together in such circumstances day after day, week after week, month after month.

I have therefore decided to go away so that you will never see me again. I have told my father that I am going to Paris with friends in order to buy my trousseau.

He will therefore not worry about me for at least two or three weeks and after that, when he cannot find me, he will have to accept that I am dead.

As our engagement has now been made public and I have

been accepted by your family, I am quite certain Papa will not do anything which will cause a scandal.

You are therefore safe and free and I can only wish you real happiness in the future.

There is one thing I would beg of you to do for me. My Stepmother threatened, when I said I had no wish to marry you, that she would have my horse taken away and starved to death and would give my dog Bracken to some man in the slums who would ill-treat him.

As I love both Swallow and Bracken more than anything else in the world, please, I beg of you, take care of them and do not let them suffer a fate they do not deserve.

Sadira.

The Earl could hardly believe that what Sadira had written about her horse and dog was true, yet he remembered the red mark on her cheek. He was well aware that the Marchioness's emotions, whether of love or hatred, lacked all control.

But how could Sadira possibly go away, presumably abroad, and disappear? He thought of how young and innocent of the world she was. If she had gone away alone, as she appeared to have done, he could not bear to think of the trouble she would find herself in. She was beautiful and, as he was well aware, every man who looked at her looked again.

He got up from his desk and walked across the room. Pacing backwards and forwards he tried to think of what he should do. He told himself that perhaps she had not gone away alone.

If she had told her father that she was going with friends to Paris, then she had probably left England with them.

The best thing he could do therefore was to try and prevent her from leaving them and going off on her own.

He ordered his carriage, then went upstairs to change from his riding-clothes. When he had done so he hurried down, aware that it was getting on for ten o'clock.

He drove to Langbourne House and asked to see the Marquess. To his relief he learned from the Butler that he was in his study alone. This meant, the Earl thought, that the Marchioness had not yet come downstairs and there was no chance of him seeing her.

The Butler opened the study door and announced him.

The Marquess, who was sitting at his desk, looked up in surprise. "Good-morning, Norwin!" he said.

"Good-morning," the Earl answered. "I have called to see you because I have had a note from Sadira."

The Marquess smiled. "I thought she would write to you too. I have had a note from her saying that she has left for Paris. I suppose no young woman can resist buying her trousseau there."

"What she omitted to tell me," the Earl said, "is her address, and of course I want to write to her."

"I can understand that," the Marquess replied, "but you will hardly believe it, she has not told me either with whom she is travelling."

He turned over some of his papers. "See for yourself," he said, and handed the Earl Sadira's note.

The Earl took it to the window and read it with his back to the Marquess.

To her father Sadira had written:

Dearest Papa,

You left earlier last night than I expected, and I did not have a chance to tell you that I have been asked to go to Paris early to-morrow morning with some friends of mine. I thought it was a marvellous opportunity to buy some beautiful gowns for my trousseau, which I am afraid will be expensive.

I know you will understand that I want to look my best to please Norwin's family who have been so sweet and kind to me.

I have therefore taken some money from your secret safe.

Take care of yourself, dearest Papa. You know that I love you and will miss you all the time I am away.

Good-bye,

Your loving daughter,

Sadira.

The Earl read the note through slowly and carefully. It was what he expected, but at the same time it was a blow since it gave him no more information than he had already.

He walked back to the desk. "As you say," he remarked to the Marquess, "there is no address, and I suppose you have no idea who these friends are?"

"I am afraid not," the Marquess answered. "It may be somewhat remiss of me, but in fact I have not met many of Sadira's friends since she left her finishing school."

The Earl thought it would be a mistake to press him. Instead he said, "Well, I am sure she will write to me as soon as she reaches Paris, and if you get a letter in the meantime, perhaps you will let me know."

"Of course I will," the Marquess promised. "It is worrying that she should have been so foolish as not to leave more details, but I expect she was in a hurry to pack. I have learned from my Butler that she had already left the house before her lady's-maid called her."

The Earl thought this was no help either.

He then forced himself to talk briefly about other things before he went back to his carriage which was waiting outside. As the horses turned round he had an idea.

Yesterday, on the way home from the luncheon, Sadira had stopped to call on a friend in Belgrave Square. That might be one of the friends with whom she had left England. At least it was an idea worth exploring.

He therefore drove to 29 Belgrave Square and asked to see Miss Beecham. He was shown by the Butler into a Sitting-Room on the ground floor.

He waited only a few minutes before Anne came in. She had been informed by the Butler who her caller was.

He saw by the expression on her face that she was surprised to see him alone. Before he could introduce himself, she asked, "Is Sadira not with you?"

"No," the Earl replied. "I have come to ask your help because Sadira has left London and not given me her address."

"Left London?" Anne exclaimed. "She said nothing about leaving when she came here yesterday!"

"I think she has gone to the country," the Earl said, "but I have no idea if she is coming back tonight or tomorrow. I am arranging a party and wish to get hold of her immediately."

"Oh!" Anne exclaimed, "then I expect she has gone to Langbourne Hall. If so, I am sure it is because she wants to see *Swallow*, her horse, and *Bracken*, her dog. Her Stepmother will not let her have them with her in London and I know how much she misses them."

"Then I certainly hope she will be back this evening," the Earl said. "but I just wondered if she had said anything about her movements to you."

"No, she came to see me about Father Christopher," Anne answered.

She saw by the expression in the Earl's eyes that the name meant nothing to him, so she explained. "Father Christopher is a Medical Missionary whom Mama has been helping. He has been doing some miraculous work in Africa, and is leaving to-day for Morocco. Both Sadira and I promised to collect some money to help him."

"That is very kind of you," the Earl said, "and of course I would like to contribute."

Anne smiled. "That is generous, but I thought it was your money that Sadira said she was taking to Father Christopher before he left."

"You say he is leaving to-day?" the Earl questioned.

Anne looked at the clock. "He will have gone by now. Some of Mama's friends were seeing him off at Tilbury. His ship was sailing at ten o'clock. I suppose now Sadira and I will have to send the money we have collected for him."

"I am sure if you give it to the Moroccan Embassy it will reach him safely," the Earl said.

"Mama can arrange all that," Anne answered lightly, "and please tell Sadira to come as soon as she can to tell me how much she has collected."

"I will," the Earl answered, "and thank you for your help."

"I am afraid I have not been very helpful," Anne said,

"but if you are having a party tonight I am sure Sadira would not want to miss it."

The Earl said good-bye and drove straight to Tilbury Docks. This took him some time because the traffic was heavy through the City. When he arrived he questioned the Dock Officials.

He learned that a cargo ship, the *Idris*, had left Tilbury for Tangier punctually at ten o'clock. Aboard it had been the Medical Missionary known as "Father Christopher".

The Earl asked if they had knowledge of the other passengers travelling on the *Idris*. All he learnt was that it was carrying a cargo of wood and was registered in Tangier. The Captain was a Scotsman, but most of the crew were Arabs.

"There are not many English travellers aboard a cargo-boat as a rule," one official said. "The cabins are often full when they arrive with Africans wishing to come to England. But going back there's usually only a handful of people making the voyage which, as you might imagine, M'Lord, is somewhat uncomfortable."

"That is what I expected," the Earl replied.

He was thinking of it all the way back to Kensall House. He was convinced that Sadira had sailed that morning on the *Idris*, and had somehow attached herself to this Father Christopher. There was no proof of it, but his instinct told him for certain that it was so.

How was it possible for anyone who had always lived luxuriously to tolerate the discomfort of a cargo-ship? Or the sort of people Sadira would encounter on such a journey? Especially as he was well aware that men of

Arab blood were attracted to women with fair hair and white skins.

He found himself clenching his fists at the thought of what might happen to Sadira. Then he remembered that Father Christopher was a Missionary, and he could only hope and pray that he would look after her.

Sadira reached Tilbury as she had hoped a little before eight o'clock. The roads were clear and the two excellent horses pulling the carriage made the journey in good time. Britan made enquiries at which quay they would find the *Idris* and they drove towards it.

Because it was so early Sadira saw with relief that there was no sign of Lady Beecham's friends. There were only men stacking heavy planks of wood onto the deck of a large, dirty and dilapidated-looking cargo-boat. Britan called to a boy who was lounging about on the quay-side to come and hold his horses, then he got down himself to open the carriage door for Sadira.

"Be this the ship ye be a-sailin' on, M'Lady?" he asked. "It don' seem t'right place for ye."

"It is going to Tangier," Sadira said, "and I only hope they have a cabin for me."

"D'ye mean as ye ain't booked one?" Britan enquired.

"No, I have not," Sadira admitted.

"Then ye'd best let Oi do t'talkin' for ye," Britan said. "Oi don't trust them Arabs not t'sting ye. They don' un'stand that as don' bargain in this country."

Sadira suddenly felt helpless. It was one thing to think she could run away and disappear for ever with Father Christopher, but it was quite another to be confronted with what was very far from her idea of a passenger-ship.

It had never struck her that the crew would be Arabs, and she could see them working and she knew that they had little respect for women.

There was every chance now that, having got as far as this, she might have to go home again. On an impulse she said to Britan, "Please . . . help me! I am travelling with a Missionary called . . . Father Christopher. He is not here yet . . . and actually he does not . . . know that I am . . . going with . . . him."

Britain stared at her. Then he said: "Oi s'pose ye know wot ye're a-doin', M'Lady, but it don' sound roight t'me!"

"Please . . . do not keep calling me 'M'Lady'," Sadira said quickly. "I have been thinking as we came here that I would call myself by my own name, but without my title and spelling it differently. You understand that I do not want anybody to be able to trace me here."

"Oi thinks as 'ow ye be runnin' away," Britan answered, "an' Oi only 'opes it's wiv some nice gen'man as'll look after ye."

"No, Britan, I am going on my own," Sadira said. "I have . . . to go so . . . please . . . please help me."

She sounded so pathetic.

Britan stopped arguing and lifted her canvas bags out of the carriage. He put them down on the ground, then said to the boy who was standing by the horses, "Now ye keep 'old o' them 'orses fer me, an' see they don't move! Oi'll pay ye fer yer pains wen Oi comes back."

"Oi'll tak' care o' them," the boy said, "Oi likes 'orses." He was patting them as he spoke.

As if Britan knew he could trust him he walked off without saying any more. Carrying Sadira's bags he climbed the gang-plank, and Sadira followed him as he pushed through a door which led to the accommodation. There was a room with a glass window which Sadira knew on a larger vessel would indicate the Purser's Office.

Britan walked up to it. There was no sign of anyone, so he knocked with his fist asking loudly, "Be there anyone at 'ome?"

An unshaven man who was obviously an Arab appeared from the back to say in broken English, "Captain on bridge. What you want?"

"Oi wants a cabin for this lady," Britan replied, "and it 'ad better be a good 'un."

The Arab found a dirty, torn piece of paper. On it was marked a number of squares which obviously represented the cabins. Some had a cross on them which told Sadira they were already engaged.

The Arab was looking for a pen and she whispered to Britan, "Ask where Father Christopher is sleeping."

He nodded and when the Arab came back he said, "This lady's workin' wi' Father Christopher an' wants to be next t' him. Where's 'is cabin?"

The Arab pointed with his finger to a square which appeared to be on the Upper Deck. "Then the lady'll 'ave the one next t' 'im." Britan persisted.

"That cabin for two," the Arab replied.

Britan was about to ask for a single cabin when Sadira said again in a whisper, "I will pay for a double cabin if it means I can have one to myself."

It was then the bargaining began. The Arab clearly understood English better than he could speak it, though he answered in monosyllables. Yet he was very sure of what he wanted.

Sadira knew Britan had been right in his assumption that the man would ask far more than he expected finally to get, but at last they came to a compromise.

Sadira produced the money which the Arab quickly grabbed. It told her that although Britan had beaten him down, she was still paying more than the going rate. The Arab came out of the office and took them along a narrow passage.

Sadira was beginning to be afraid of what she might be confronted with. To her relief, however, when the cabin door was opened it was small but clean; and fortunately it was also not an inside cabin and had a port-hole. The two bunks took up most of the room with only a very narrow space between them.

She was just about to say that she was content with the cabin when Britan exclaimed, "There be nothin' on them beds! Wot about blankets?"

The Arab grinned. "You pay," he said.

Once again they were haggling, but before they had got very far Britan insisted that he should see the blankets. The Arab went from the cabin and beckoned.

"Ye stay 'ere," Britan said to Sadira, "an' leave this t'me."

He went away and Sadira sat down on one of the bunks, thinking how foolish she had been. She should have noticed that while both bunks had coarse straw mattresses on them there were no pillows or blankets, nor were there any rugs on the rough wooden floor.

She was waiting. There was the sound of the men stacking wood and shouting to each other as they did so. Suddenly she began to feel frightened.

Was she really brave enough, she asked herself, to carry out her plan and leave England never to return? Would it not be better to marry the Earl? Then she thought of her Stepmother.

It would be preferable even to be alone and defenceless in an Arab city. Anything would be better than being aware of the hatred that vibrated towards her every time she met her Stepmother.

She was deep in her thoughts when Britan returned. He was smiling and carrying two blankets. The Arab held two others in his arms.

The man threw them down on one of the bunks. Sadira held out some money towards Britan and he took it from her, giving it to the Arab.

It must have been to his satisfaction because he beamed and even made Sadira a slight *salaam* before he left the cabin.

"Thank you for doing that for me," Sadira said to Britan. "It was quick of you to notice there were no blankets on the bunks."

"They ain't got no sheets," Britan said, "but them blankets be new an' clean. Some of wot 'e showed me Oi wouldn't let a dog sleep on!"

"I am very grateful," Sadira said.

"They didn't 'ave no pillows either," Britan went on, "so Oi got ye an extra blanket as ye can roll up an' put under ye 'ead. Ye'll be quite comfortable."

"I am sure I shall," Sadira replied. "And thank you, thank you very much again. I could not have . . . done it without . . . you."

She pressed some money into his hand, doubling what she had intended to give him before they started.

He thanked her and turned towards the door. "Ye tak' care o' yerself," he said, "an' if things don't work out come 'ome. Oi never did trust these 'ere foreigners! An Oi wouldn't trust this lot any further than Oi could throw 'em!"

"I will be all right," Sadira answered, "and thank you once again."

She held out her hand and Britan shook it. "God bless ye, M'Lady," he said, "and if ye asks me ye'll need 'im lookin' after ye."

When he had gone Sadira shut the cabin door. She went to the port-hole hoping she would be able to see the Quay. She could see at least part of it.

Since she had come on board she knew that quite a number of other people had arrived, but she was not certain whether they were passengers or those getting the ship ready for the voyage.

She could however see Britan driving away. As he did so she felt she was losing her last contact with the world she knew. She opened the port-hole wider to let in some fresh air, and by standing on tip-toe and poking her head out she had a better view of the quay than she had before.

Now she could just glimpse the gangway up which she had come, and she knew it was to be used only by the passengers, for there was another further along the ship's side for those working aboard.

Time went by, then she was aware that carriages were arriving. She was sure some of them would contain Lady Beecham's friends who had come to see Father Christopher off and give him what money they had already collected.

It was a relief when she was certain that he was aboard. She had a sudden fear that, despite the fact that his cabin was booked, he might change his plan at the last moment. In which case, she knew she would be too frightened to go on alone.

Another carriage arrived. Now she saw Father Christopher getting out of it, accompanied by another man who was wearing a cassock. He did not look as if he was a traveller and Sadira thought he was another missionary seeing Father Christopher off.

As soon as Father Christopher appeared the ladies waiting got out of their carriages. They clustered around him and Sadira could see they were all giving him small parcels.

Then she was aware that two of the ladies carried baskets on their arms, and it struck her that perhaps she should have brought some food with her. She thought it was very foolish not to think of it before.

Finally, after a great deal of conversation, Father Christopher started to climb up the gangway. He had said good-bye to most of the ladies. Two who were laden with his gifts climbed up the gangplank after him.

Now Sadira could not see him, but a few minutes later she heard his deep voice and the high-pitched chattering of the ladies' voices in the cabin next to hers.

She could hear quite clearly what they were saying, so she realised there was only a thin partition between them. "I hope we have thought of everything you will need, Father," one of the ladies remarked.

"You have been more than kind," Father Christopher replied, "and I am very grateful indeed for all you have given me, especially the money which will be used for those who most need it."

"We shall be thinking of you, Father, and collecting more which we will send to you through the Embassy."

"God will bless you for your generosity," Father Christopher replied.

There was more chatter, then Sadira heard a voice calling, "All ashore! All ashore!"

"We must go!" one of the ladies cried. "Good-bye, dear Father, and remember us in your prayers."

"You may be quite certain I will do that," Father Christopher promised. He said good-bye a dozen more times before Sadira heard the ladies hurrying away, and she thought Father Christopher had followed them.

She heard the engines start up and a few minutes later the ship began to move. Looking out of the port-hole Sadira could see the ladies waving their handkerchiefs.

She knew that Father Christopher would be waving to them from the deck.

The ship increased its speed and the quay was now out of sight. Sadira went back to sit on the side of one of the bunks. Now that she was actually leaving England she felt really frightened, for suppose Father Christopher refused to take her and put her ashore before they reached the open sea. She was not quite certain how he could do that, but it was a possibility.

She therefore decided it would be wise not to reveal her presence until it was impossible for him to send her home. She heard him go into his cabin and close the door behind him.

She made up her bunk with the clean, unused blankets which Britan had found for her, and took off her jacket and hung the cape she had brought with her on a hook on the wall.

Although it was hot at the moment, she thought that perhaps when they reached the Bay of Biscay it might be cold. She had therefore brought with her a travelling-cape, which had belonged to her mother and was lined with fur. She had packed only her plainest clothes, but the cape was an exception, for she thought it would be a mistake to shiver.

The ship had now reached the Straits of Dover and was rolling a little. Sadira lay down on her bunk.

She put her head, as Britan had suggested, on a rolled up blanket and it was quite comfortable. She decided to wait for at least an hour before she went to see Father Christopher. Actually she was very frightened of doing so, as he might be angry, and might,when they reached Tangier, insist upon sending her back on the next ship that was going to England.

Then she remembered that he had no jurisdiction over her. What was more, she had the money she had taken from her father's safe. "I must be very careful that it is not stolen from me," she thought, then shivered.

It was no use pretending even to herself that

everything did not depend on Father Christopher. She had met him only once, but now she was asking him to take her under his protection. "Please . . . please, God, make him do . . . that," she prayed.

CHAPTER SIX

Sadira was tired by the time they reached Fez, which was not surprising. She expected to have a quiet time on the *Idris* as long as Father Christopher accepted her as being there.

When she first approached him he was very surprised. But he accepted her decision to leave home without argument.

She thought it was wonderful of him, especially when he said, "You have come as my student, and that is what you must be. If you have to look after yourself you will be safer with Missionaries like me and working with them."

"That is what I want," Sadira answered, "and thank you, thank you for understanding."

"I do not say I approve," Father Christopher replied, "but we all have to live our own lives and, if it is God's will, then you will succeed in what you have undertaken."

As his student, Sadira was astonished to find how much there was to do, especially as Father Christopher was the only person with any medical knowledge aboard the ship. So he was busy, Sadira found, from first thing in the morning until last thing at night. Men who had carried the cargo of wood on board had injured their hands, their shoulders, then feet, and they all asked for treatment.

Then before they had got very far into the Bay of Biscay there was a violent storm. One seaman broke an arm, another his leg. Father Christopher set both very skillfully, and Sadira had to help him with the bandaging and the plaster which fortunately he had brought with him.

In fact one large trunk was filled with nothing but medical supplies which Father Christopher was taking to Fez, though quite a lot of these had to be used on the voyage. By the time they sailed into the Port of Tangier Sadira was priding herself on becoming quite expert at nursing.

Father Christopher was anxious to get to Fez as quickly as possible to discover why they needed him. He therefore hired horses rather than mules, and they set off with a caravan of Arabs to assist them.

The horses carried small tents in which Sadira and Father Christopher could sleep at night. It fascinated her how quickly the tents could be erected and dismantled. But the countryside through which they were passing was not particularly interesting, and she was glad that they did not stay in the small towns and villages they passed.

The ground at first was parched and cracked. A few hawks swayed lazily in the sky and occasionally they disturbed a brilliantly coloured goldfinch. Then they rode over marshy plains and later past a few forests or cork trees.

It took them twelve days to reach Fez. Before they got to the City Father Christopher told Sadira that it had been built in about A.D. 800. "Fez the Devout," he said, "is one of the most revered religious centres of the Moslem world, but it is not now as powerful as it was in the past. Today far too many people live there. In fact, there are nearly 200,000 inhabitants in the Old City alone."

Sadira did not envisage quite what they really meant until they reached Fez.

Late in the evening they descended the steep, narrow and sunless passages which were not really worthy of being called streets.

They passed the Qarawiyin Mosque which she was told could accommodate 22,000 worshipers, but only Moslems were admitted.

Then at last, when it was almost too dark to see the way, they stopped in a tiny square, where the houses looked rough and in need of repair. Sadira could not believe they were going to stay there, but Father Christopher said with a sigh of satisfaction, "We have arrived!"

As he spoke the door of one house opened and a stream of people came running out. They were waving their hands in welcome and talking at the tops of their voices.

During the voyage in the *Idris*, Sadira had learned a little Arabic both from Father Christopher and from his patients. She was aware that the people were all thanking God that he had reached them safely. She also thought they were expecting him to solve all their problems, whatever they might be.

They had ridden all day with hardly a stop for anything to eat, so as Sadira dismounted she thought the only thing she needed was a bed in which to sleep.

She had however first to partake of a large meal which had been prepared for Father Christopher. The people had been making ready for whatever day he arrived, and they never stopped talking for a moment.

She learned later that they were all Christians, and it was because they were having a difficult time with the Moslems that they were so anxious for Father Christopher to join them.

The house, built mostly of wood, was very primitive. As she might have expected, they all sat on the floor with the food spread out in front of them. The main dish was *kouskous*, made with a kind of semolina topped with a savoury stew, which was surprisingly palatable.

Sadira also liked the almond and honey cakes which were always served, she learned, at a meal in Morocco.

Since arriving at Tangier she had become accustomed to eating with her fingers. She learned that Moroccans thought to use cutlery was a very dirty way of eating.

After the meal was over she was able to go up the rickety staircase, and was shown into a small room in which there was a divan raised about six inches from the floor, on which there was a deep and comfortable mattress.

She was too tired to take anything out of her bags except for her nightgown. Her last thought before she lay down was that in this strange, rabbit-like warren off a city there would be a great number of injured or sick people, who would all need Father Christopher's skills. Tomorrow and all the days that followed were likely to be very busy.

Below, Father Christopher was being plied with questions as to why he had brought an English girl with him. "She is my disciple," he said firmly and refused to add any more information.

Outside the Old City, in the impressive and luxurious Palace of the Sultan, the Earl had been waiting for nearly a week.

When he left Tilbury he was convinced that he knew where Sadira had gone. He had returned to Kensall House, and there he sent for his Secretary, Mr. Barratt, whom he informed that he was leaving England at once in his yacht which was in Dover Harbour.

Mr. Barrett was appalled.

"How can you do that, My Lord?" he asked. "You have a great number of important engagements – two with His Royal Highness. The Prime Minister is expecting you at a Conference which he is holding on Thursday."

He paused and then continued, "And there are also the parties you have arranged for your relatives to meet Lady Sadira."

"I know that," the Earl agreed, "and you will somehow have to cover up for me." He paused as if in deep thought and then continued, "Tell His Royal Highness and the Prime Minister that I am visiting a relative who is dying, and tell my relatives that the Prime Minister has sent me abroad on an urgent mission."

He paused again and then said, "In fact I am leaving for Fez as soon as I can reach *The Mermaid*."

This was the name of the Earl's yacht, which was always expected to be in readiness for him to leave England at short notice, though he had not used it for at least three months.

Mr. Barratt was told to send a warning to the Captain of his Master's imminent arrival, and he was also given the task of saving Sadira's horse, *Swallow*. The Earl told him to get the animal removed from the stables of Langbourne Hall together with *Bracken*, the dog, and have them taken to Kensall Park.

Leaving Mr. Barratt gasping with the number of other orders, he ran upstairs to supervise his packing.

Hopkins, his Valet, was used to his Master making quick decisions and expecting them to be carried out at the double.

He had been his batman in the Army, and this had taught him how to cope with considerable dexterity with any emergency. His duties had involved much travelling on the Continent and in other parts of the world, so he was now delighted at the opportunity of getting away from the humdrum routine in England.

Even by the Earl's standards it seemed as if his luggage was packed and ready with the wave of a magic wand.

The Earl drove his Four-in-Hand towards the coast with Hopkins sitting behind him. Thanks to Mr.

Barratt's efficient organisation, *The Mermaid* was alerted in good time, and the ship moved out of harbour the minute the Earl stepped aboard.

As he went up on the bridge to be with the Captain, the Earl felt glad to be leaving London behind. For the moment he would be no longer worried by the problem of the Marchioness, although of course there would be the Marquess's distress when he could not find Sadira.

"How can she have thought of anything so fantastic as disappearing completely?" the Earl asked himself.

At the same time he could not help admiring her courage in taking the initiative. He could understand her violent revulsion from a situation which was so abhorrent to her, and he knew, if he was honest, that it was the sort of thing he would have done himself.

It seemed extraordinary however that one small, rather fragile-looking girl could run away. Could she really believe that she could live her own life without anybody trying to find her? "It is a crazy idea!" the Earl said scornfully.

And yet he could not help thinking it was a very brave one.

The Bay of Biscay proved to be just as uncomfortable for *The Mermaid* as it had been for the *Idris*.

Sadira had not been seasick, because there had been so many casualties she had been too busy to think about herself. Just the same happened on *The Mermaid*.

Three seamen were injured during a storm, and the Earl took the Captain's place on the bridge while he attended to them. He was not as skilful as Father Christopher, but they were hobbling about a few days later.

Having learnt from the officials at Tilbury that the *Idris* was going to Tangier, the Earl decided to put into the port of Rabat, as it was a little nearer to Fez and it took him only nine days to reach the outskirts of the City.

Here he was fortunate in finding two good horses for himself and his Valet, though his luggage had to be carried by mules and this caused them to slow down. However when he arrived in Fez he went straight to the Sultan's Palace.

He had stayed with the Sultan on a previous visit some four years earlier, and had also entertained the Sultan when he visited London. He therefore knew that he would be welcome, and he had told Mr. Barratt to advise the Moroccan Embassy of his intention and to get in touch with the Sultan.

He learned on arrival that they had sent a courier overland to inform the Sultan of his arrival, so the Earl was received with delight. The Sultan, who was a comparatively young man, immediately started to talk to him about his horses, and it was such a familiar conversation that it seemed as if they had picked it up just where they had left off.

It was quite a while before the Earl was able to explain why he had come to Fez. He told the Sultan that he wished to get in touch with the Missionary, Father Christopher. The Sultan immediately gave instructions that the Earl was to be told as soon as he was known to have arrived.

The Earl knew it might be a number of days before this happened, so he relaxed and enjoyed himself.

The Sultan was very intelligent and had surrounded himself with some of the best brains in Morocco. The

luncheons and dinners he gave for the Earl were attended
of course entirely by men, and there was no question of
any of the women in the Sultan's Harem eating with
them.

It was very hot in the daytime, but cool at night, and
there were a number of interesting things in Fez the Earl
had not seen on his last visit.

The days passed, but when there was no news of
Father Christopher the Earl began to grow impatient.
He wondered if, after all, the Missionary had not made
his way to Fez, for he might instead have chosen to linger
in some other town, and there were one or two on the
route which, as the Earl knew, would welcome a medical
man.

The day after Sadira arrived, the Earl and the Sultan
had gone to a Camel Market which had taken place some
way outside the City. Here it had been very interesting to
watch the camels being sold, and there were also a
number of horses for sale which the Earl inspected
carefully before advising the Sultan which ones were, in
his opinion, the best.

They celebrated the success of the Market with the
man who had arranged it, and were late arriving back at
the Palace where the Earl went to his room to change for
dinner.

He thought as he did so that he was growing bored
with eating *shish kebab* and deep baked chicken *tajine*.
Also a steaming mountain of *kouskous*, which was prepared in Fez and contained cinnamon and sweet yellow
raisins. He also felt iritated by the small plates of peppery
condiments, olives, nuts and sweetmeats.

What he really wanted was a glass of champagne rather than the scalding, intensely sweet, green mint tea. Nevertheless he knew that was what would be waiting for him when he went downstairs.

He knew what was upsetting him was the fact that he had not yet found Sadira.

He finished his meal with the Sultan, and as he did so one of the servants, first making an obeisance, informed him that Father Christopher had arrived the previous evening.

"Why was His Lordship not informed immediately?" the Sultan demanded angrily.

The man explained with embarrassment that they had been watching the main entrance into the City. Father Christopher, he said, had entered by a less important one.

The Sultan was extremely annoyed that his orders had not been carried out efficiently enough. The Earl however was greatly relieved.

He thanked him for a delicious meal and asked that he could have a Guide. He would be taken immediately to wherever Father Christopher was staying.

The moon was shining brightly as he left so that it was easy to see the way to the entrance of the Old City. Then they were walking through the narrow passages where the moon could not percolate and it was very dark. Although it was growing late the passages were crowded with people. There were children carrying wooden trays of bread dough on their heads, and women doing the family wash at an exquisitely tiled public fountain, with bearded old men selling caged birds.

The old Berber ladies with tatooed chins squatted on

the kerbs with their hands held out as they begged, whilst there were also numbers of ragged porters dragging or pushing slow-moving monkeys loaded down with sheepskins.

The Earl followed his Guide. He was wearing the long djellaba with its sharply peaked hood like all the other men they passed.

The night air was clamorous with rhythmic hammerings as the iron workers were busy on their kettles. There were coppersmiths, tap-tapping on ornate trays, and the continual sound of the high voices of the street vendors.

The Guide twisted in and out of the passages, apparently well aware of where he was going. They were moving swiftly, and as they went deeper and deeper into the Old City, they were continually interrupted by the cry, "*Balek! Balek!*"

The Earl knew already that this meant "Make way!" He moved quickly into a doorway as a donkey came round the corner. It usually carried so much on its back that whatever the load it swept against the Earl's chest as it passed.

Then the Guide was off again, and they were moving through an aroma of spices and newly-cut cedarwood, or singed ox-horn and hot cooking-oil.

The Earl began to think they must have reached the very bottom of the hill on which the City was built when there was suddenly a flaring light ahead.

The Guide turned his head to say, "Fire, Excellency – house on fire!"

The Earl knew this often happened in Fez, for the majority of the houses were built of wood. They walked on. Now the Earl saw in front of him a small square with a fountain in the centre of it. On the far side a crowd had collected to stare at one of the houses out of whose doors and windows flames were leaping.

The Guide kept going forwards towards it, and the Earl followed. As they drew nearer still he was suddenly afraid that this might be the house in which Sadira was staying. Even as he thought of it, he saw a white-haired man, taller than the crowd around him, who was wearing a cassock.

The Earl struggled to reach him, but the crowd was too thick. As he moved he saw several women being brought out through the door of the burning house. As one of them was supported outside she screamed, "My baby! My baby! It is left behind! My baby!" Her voice rose to a shrill screech.

Then from the other side of the man with the white hair the Earl saw Sadira move forward to speak to the woman. Then she ran straight into the house from which the people had escaped.

He could hardly believe his eyes as he watched what was happening, and there was a murmur amongst the crowd, as if they protested at what Sadira had just done.

The Earl suddenly realised that he was just standing, staring at the flaming house. Quickly he pulled off his coat and said to his Guide, "Give me your *djellaba*."

The Guide took it off and thrust it into the Earl's arms. Moving to the fountain he dipped the *djellaba* into the water, and when it was soaked he lifted it out dripping with water, and put it on.

"Now I want another one," he said sharply.

This the Guide translated into Arabic and a man standing near the Earl understood. He pulled off the *djellaba* he was wearing and thrust it into the fountain. The Earl snatched it from him.

As the people moved aside he ran into the burning building after Sadira. Inside the centre of it was not burning so violently as the outer walls.

There was a staircase in front of him, and he was about to climb it, thinking the baby Sadira had gone to rescue would be on the first floor, when there was a crash and the staircase collapsed in flames.

It was then, as the Earl stared in dismay, that he saw Sadira. She had come from a back room behind the staircase. As the staircase collapsed she stopped and looked upwards, and the Earl knew she was praying. The leaping flames seemed suddenly to encircle her enveloping her in a halo of light. Just for a second the Earl looked at her with the baby held close to her heart. Then he ran forward and without speaking threw the soaking *djellaba* over her, covering her head with the hood.

He lifted her and the baby up into his arms. "Hide your face against me!" he ordered.

As he felt her obey him he moved towards the door, for the fire by now had complete control of the house. The Earl knew that the only thing he could do would be to rush his way through it.

Holding Sadira very tightly in his arms, he bent his head and took a deep breath, then he crashed through the flames and out into the darkness beyond them.

As he did so the crowd started cheering. When he

reached them a dozen hands beat out the flames, which despite the wetness of the *djellaba* had started to burn the cotton. Aware that he was outside and still alive, the Earl pushed back the hood over his head.

Gently he removed the *djellaba* covering Sadira which had concealed the baby from the crowd. When they saw that he had rescued them both they cheered again, and the mother of the child went down on her knees before the Earl.

She kissed his feet before she rose to take the baby from Sadira's arms with the tears running down her cheeks.

"He . . . is . . . all right . . . He is . . . not . . . hurt," Sadira said in a trembling voice which seemed to come from a long distance.

As if to confirm her words the baby started to cry. His mother clutched him against her.

The Earl threw off his *djellaba*, then once again picked Sadira up in his arms. "I will take you home," he said.

She shut her eyes and rested her head against his shoulder, too overcome and shocked by what had happened to be able to reply. Father Christopher came to the Earl's side.

"I can only thank God," he said, "that you were here and that your bravery has saved Sadira when I thought it impossible for her to survive."

"I am taking her now to the Palace," the Earl said, "and I would like to see you in the morning."

"Of course," Father Christopher replied.

With Sadira in his arms the Earl followed the Guide who was leading the way back. The crowd made way for them to pass and get away from the burning house. Once again they were in the narrow passages, but this time moving uphill instead of down, and although it was a long way back to the Palace the Earl found Sadira was very light.

Too light and too fragile, he thought, to have committed such an act of courage. For he knew that if he had not been there she must have been burned to death.

They reached the gateway of the Old City, and now that it was easy to see by the light of the moon Sadira said, "I . . . I think I can . . . walk now."

"There is no need for you to do so," the Earl answered, "and the sooner you can rest, after what you have been through, the better."

"H.how could . . . you be . . . there . . . how could you . . . suddenly appear . . . when I thought . . . both the . . . baby and I must . . . d.die?"

"I will tell you about it tomorrow," the Earl replied. "Now you are going to be the guest of the Sultan, and I think you will find it very much more comfortable than where you have been staying."

She looked up at him in surprise, and the light of the moon was on her face. The Earl thought no-one could be more beautiful, yet at the same time somehow pathetic and in need of protection.

He did not say any more as they walked through the Palace garden and into the great building itself. The Guide had gone ahead of them talking in his own language to explain to the servants what had happened. One of them, obviously with some authority, led the way upstairs, and the Earl carried Sadira into what he knew was one of the best guest rooms.

There was a luxurious divan on which to sleep, and cushions on which to sit were set out on an exquisite carpet. Very gently he put Sadira down on the bed.

She was wearing, he saw, only a simple muslin gown which he was aware would have burnt quickly if the flames had caught it. She looked up at him. Her face was very pale, but there was a smile on her lips.

For a moment they were alone in the room while the manservant went to fetch women to attend to her."Is it . . . really true that you are . . . h.here and . . . and you have . . . saved me?" Sadira whispered.

"It is true," the Earl answered. As he spoke he bent forward and kissed her gently on the lips.

Then the women came hurrying into the room, chattering loudly at the horror of what had happened.

The Earl straightened himself and moved away from the bed. Just for a second his eyes met Sadira's.

Then, knowing there was nothing more he could do, he went towards the door.

CHAPTER SEVEN

Hopkins called the Earl at his usual time. When he had drawn back the curtains he said, "There's a letter, M'Lord, come from th' Embassy."

He put it down on the bed and the Earl picked it up. He recognised at once his Secretary's handwriting and wondered what could be so urgent that he had written again.

Barratt had already written to say that Sadira's horse and her dog had been removed from Langbourne Hall to Kensall Park, and that they were settling down quite happily.

The Earl opened the letter and the first words he read made him stiffen.

Barratt had written:

"My Lord,

I am writing to tell you that the newspapers have today announced the death of the Marchioness of Langbourne resulting from a regrettable shooting accident which involved Lord Cairn."

The Earl drew in his breath. He knew Lord Cairn, who was an eccentric who was a member of White's Club. It amused him when he went out at night to carry a revolver and when he was approached by footpads, which was inevitable around Piccadilly, he would draw his revolver and confront them with it.

When, terrified, they ran away he would fire harmlessly into the air or onto the ground after them, which caused them to run even quicker. He greatly enjoyed this, although the Earl and the other members of the Club considered it undignified.

Mr. Barratt continued, *". . . Because I thought Your Lordship would want to know the full circumstances I got in touch with the Butler. He told me – of course in the strictest confidence – that the Marquess had gone away for the night, but returned home unexpectedly.*

He found Her Ladyship and Lord Cairn in compromising circumstances and threatened them with divorce proceedings.

Apparently Lord Cairn sprang out of bed and seizing his revolver threatened to shoot His Lordship.

Her Ladyship screamed and in an attempt to avoid a scandal tried to force up Lord Cairn's arm. Unfortunately she also pushed him and, as he had been drinking heavily, he fell backwards. In doing so, he pulled the trigger and the bullet buried itself in Her Ladyship's breast.

The Doctor was sent for, but Her Ladyship never regained consciousness and died the following morning. His Lordship is of course deeply distressed and, if Your Lordship has been successful in finding Lady Sadira, perhaps you could tell Her Ladyship.

I remain,

   Your obedient servant,

      Robert Barratt."

The Earl read the letter through twice, telling himself that, as far as he and Sadira were concerned, nothing could be more fortunate.

He could understand exactly what had happened. The Marquess, having been outwitted once, was determined not to let it occur again. He knew that Lord Cairn, besides being an eccentric, was also a heavy drinker, and it was easy therefore to see how such an accident could have happened.

While the Earl was dressing he sent Hopkins to find out if Sadira was awake.

When he came back the Valet said, "According to th' maids as looking after Her Ladyship she's sleepin' like a baby M'Lord. If you asks me, it's the best thing Her Ladyship could do."

"I agree with you," the Earl said. 'Tell them I am going driving with the Sultan, but they are to insist that Her Ladyship stays in bed and rests. She should not attempt to get up today."

"I'll tell 'em, M'Lord," Hopkins replied, "but I 'spect it's what they'll be thinking themselves. They're a lazy lot when Your Lordship compares 'em to what English ladies do."

The Earl smiled, but did not reply. When he had finished dressing and had breakfast he knew the Sultan would be waiting for him.

Sadira stirred and felt as if she was coming back to life through a very dark tunnel. She thought she must have slept all through the night. When she opened her eyes she saw the sunshine streaming in through the windows, and for a moment she could not think where she was.

Then she remembered what had happened last night and how the Earl had saved her. "How can he have come to Fez at all, and just at the right moment?" she asked herself.

When she had found the baby in the back room she had come out just as the staircase collapsed. It had spread the fire all over the ground floor and the front wall of the house was a mass of flames. It seemed to her there was nothing that was not on fire.

She thought that both she and the baby in her arms must be burned to death. "Help me ... help me ... God!" she prayed.

At that moment she had seen a tall figure shrouded in a *djellaba* coming towards her. The robe he wore disguised him, but she knew instinctively who it was. Her prayer had been answered.

She only knew as he covered her with the wet *djellaba* and picked her up in his arms that she need no longer be afraid. She had hidden her face against his shoulder as he told her to do, and later, as he carried her along the twisting streets, she had felt herself drifting away.

There was no fear; only a feeling of safety and thankfulness that she was still alive.

She thought now she must have been hardly conscious when the Earl had carried her into the Palace and up the stairs. He had set her down on the bed and she looked up at him.

Then he had bent his head and kissed her.

She could still feel, as she thought of it, the sudden shaft of ecstasy which had run through her. It was like nothing she had known before.

She told herself now that he had only kissed her as he might have kissed a child. But there had been nothing childlike in what she felt. Although she hardly dared to admit it to herself, she knew she wanted him to kiss her again.

She lay thinking of the Earl just as a man; not worrying as to why he was here or how he had found her.

She was drifting again in a dream world which made her feel very happy. A short time later the woman peeped in to see if she was awake. Sadira raised her head to ask the time and was told it was midday.

"How can I have slept for so long?" she asked. She knew it was a combination of the voyage, the long ride from Tangier and the terror of the fire.

The woman brought her some food to eat and exotic fruit which she enjoyed. When she suggested she should get up she told her that His Lordship had gone driving with the Sultan, and he had given orders that she was to stay in bed and rest.

Sadira had no wish to do anything else. But she felt guilty at allowing herself to be treated as an invalid when she had promised to help Father Christopher. However there were, she remembered, a great number of people in the house where she had stayed. She knew they would enjoy helping him as she had done.

It grew very hot in the afternoon and she slept again. When she awoke she was aware with a leap of her heart that she was not alone. Sitting beside her on the divan was the Earl.

She gave a little cry. "I have been asleep," she said, "and I did not know . . . you were . . . there."

"I was beginning to think that you were Mrs. Rip Van Winkle!" the Earl teased.

Sadira sat up against her pillows. She had no idea how lovely she looked with her fair hair falling over her shoulders nearly to her waist. She was wearing a diaphanous nightgown, which she had brought because she thought it was lighter than any of her others.

She did not feel self-conscious, even though she was in bed. She only thought how handsome the Earl was, and how strong and dependable he looked.

"You are all right?" he asked with a note of concern in his voice.

"I am . . . only being . . . lazy on your . . . instructions," Sadira answered. She gave a little laugh as she added, "Now that I am feeling so well I want to dance for joy because you . . . saved me and that . . . dear little baby."

"How could you do anything so reckless – yet amazingly courageous?" the Earl asked. "When I saw you running through the door and into the flames I could not believe my eyes!"

"How could I . . . let the baby . . . die?" Sadira asked, "and how could . . . you be so . . . wonderful as to be . . . there in answer to . . . my prayer?"

"I thought you were praying," the Earl said, "and it was only your prayers which got us out of that burning house."

Sadira smiled at him and he said, "I have a lot to tell you."

"I am listening and I only hope you are not very . . . angry with . . . me."

"I am not angry, but shocked and horrified that you should have run away as you did," the Earl replied. "I understood of course why you wanted to do so."

Sadira looked away from him, knowing he was referring to her Stepmother.

"Your reasoning, however," the Earl went on, "was completely wrong."

"Wrong?" Sadira queried.

"You said in your letter," the Earl said slowly, "that you thought that when we were together I was wishing there was someone else in your place. That however was not the case at all."

Sadira could not look at him and he continued, "You thought I was in love, but in fact I have never in the past been in love. That was why I was determined not to marry."

Sadira turned to look at him and her eyes were very wide. "Y.you have . . . never been in l.love?" she asked, "I . . . I do not . . . understand."

"Then let me explain it to you," the Earl said. "You think, because you are young, of love as the ideal and perfect love which we all seek, but few are privileged to find."

He saw that Sadira was looking puzzled and went on, "But while a man may seek for what he thinks of as a jewel without fault or the purity of a lily, he would be inhuman if he refused the other flowers he encountered by the roadside."

"What you are . . . saying," Sadira said hesitatingly, "is that . . . you have found . . . other women . . . attractive . . . but you did not l.love them."

"That is it exactly," the Earl agreed. "It is quite natural for a man and a woman to be attracted physically to each other. For the man it is a pleasure to make her his, and what he feels is of great satisfaction to his body, but not to his mind and soul."

He dropped his voice as he added, "What I have been seeking all my life is the love that my mother taught me is part of God. I knew that when I found the woman I really loved I would worship her."

Sadira felt herself quiver at the note in his voice as he said the last words. Before she could say anything the Earl said gently, "And that is what I felt last night when I saw you standing with the baby in your arms and the flames threatening to consume you."

"Y.you . . . saved me," Sadira managed to say.

"By the mercy of God I saved you," the Earl replied, "but, my darling, it is something you must never do again, unless you wish to destroy me."

He saw the sudden radiance that transformed Sadira's face, and reached out his hands to take hers. He felt her quiver at his touch and said very softly, "I love you! I love you with my heart and soul, and I have been searching the earth and sky for you all my life!"

"It . . . cannot be . . . true!" Sadira whispered.

"It is true!" the Earl said. "I intend to make you love

me as I love you, and to make certain that you cannot escape me again."

Sadira felt as if the sunshine dazzled her eyes. She was bemused, bewildered, and at the same time entranced by what the Earl was saying to her. It was impossible to find words to answer him.

His fingers tightened on hers as he said, "So that you can never escape me, I have arranged that in a short while Father Christopher will come here to marry us."

"To . . . marry us?"

Sadira could hardly breathe the words, but the Earl heard them.

"I am sure you know that a Missionary carries with him a consecrated stone" the Earl said. "It seems that he can administer a Holy Sacrament wherever it is needed. When I told him what I wanted he said he was very proud of you and delighted to conduct our Marriage Service."

"Are you quite . . . quite certain that . . . you want to . . . be married?"

"I am more certain than I have ever been about anything," the Earl declared. "And as I have already told you, I am taking no chances: I will not allow you to leave this bed until you are my wife!"

Unexpectedly Sadira laughed.

"I know . . . this is . . . a dream," she protested. "I ran away from England because I thought it would make you happy never to see me again, but now you are telling me we are . . . to be . . . married!"

"We will be married," the Earl affirmed, "and I know, my lovely one, we will be very happy. As you said yourself, we have our horses in common."

He saw the question in Sadira's eyes before she asked it.

"*Swallow* is waiting for you in my stables," he said, "and *Bracken* is with my dogs."

He saw her apprehension fade away. Then he said quietly, "I have some other news for you – your Stepmother is dead."

"Dead? H.how can . . . she be . . . dead?" Sadira asked in astonishment.

"I understand from a letter my Secretary sent me that it was a shooting accident."

Sadira gave a little gasp. "P.Papa did not . . . kill her?"

"No, no. It was a man called Lord Cairn who always carries a revolver and also drinks too much."

He paused and then continued, "I understand he was showing your father the pistol, but the trigger was faulty. The gun went off and the bullet struck your Stepmother."

The Earl guessed as he spoke that that was the story which would appear in the newspapers.

It was all Sadira needed to know.

He had no wish for her to receive another shock by learning the truth of what had happened. But she was more intelligent than he gave her credit for.

"Oh, poor Papa!" Sadira exclaimed. "If he has been deceived again he must be very upset."

"He is," the Earl replied, "and that is why, my darling, I think that after a short honeymoon we must go back so that you can comfort him."

Sadira felt it was wrong to be glad that her Stepmother was no longer alive, but she could not help feeling that a heavy weight had been lifted from her shoulders. There was no longer a ghastly fear at the back of her mind. A fear that if she and the Earl returned to England the Marchioness would somehow contrive to make her miserable, and would attempt to break up their marriage.

Sadira felt now as if the sunshine had suddenly become more dazzling and she could hear the angels singing.

The Earl was watching the expression on her face.

"I think" Sadira said softly, "what I am feeling is . . . love and it is . . . very . . . very wonderful."

"I will teach you to be sure that what we feel for each other is the perfect love in which we both believe," the Earl answered.

He put his arm around her shoulders. Then he was kissing her, at first gently, but later as he felt the softness and sweetness of her lips, more obsessively.

He kissed her until Sadira felt the ecstasy was beyond anything she had imagined or dreamt love would be like.

It was perfectly, incredibly wonderful!

When the Earl moved she held onto him as if she was afraid he would leave her.

"I love . . . you," she said, "I do . . . love you! Please . . . go on . . . loving me."

"You may be quite certain of that," the Earl assured her.

Then he was kissing her again.

Later there was a sound outside the door, and the Earl was aware that time was passing. He looked down for a moment at Sadira's face thinking it would be impossible for anyone to look more beautiful, or more spiritual. It was that, he knew, which had made her, from the very beginning, seem different from all other women he had known.

Now he knew that the sensations they had aroused in him were as nothing compared with the ecstasy he felt when he kissed Sadira. He rose from the divan and walked towards the door.

Outside he saw great clusters of flowers. He knew that the women were waiting to bring them into the bedroom, and thought by now Father Christopher would be arriving.

Leaving Sadira to the women, he went to find him. When the Earl reached the hall, Father Christopher was just stepping out of the carriage which had been sent for him.

Hopkins was also there, holding in his hand a sheath of Madonna Lilies. The Earl knew that to him she would always have the purity and perfection of a lily.

That again was something he had never found in any other woman.

Hopkins took Father Christopher to a room where he could put on his surplice, while the Earl went to see if Sadira was ready.

When he went into the bedroom the women all covered their faces and faded away.

The Earl stood at the foot of the divan and looked at his Bride. He had remembered to order a wreath fashioned of tiny white flowers, and now it was on her head. To him it was more becoming than any diamond tiara could have been. He put the lilies on the bed in front of her.

As she smiled at him a little shyly he knew he was the luckiest man in the world, and was prepared to challenge anyone who contradicted him.

"Thank . . . you for the lovely . . . flowers," Sadira said.

They scented the room and were massed on either side of the bed. It appeared as if Sadira was in a bower of roses, orchids and camelias.

There were no words, the Earl thought, in which to express how lovely she looked.

Then the door behind him opened and Father Christopher came in, wearing a white surplice. In one hand he carried the consecrated stone, in the other he held a Prayer Book.

He put the stone down on the table beside the bed. Then, opening his Prayer Book, he began the Marriage Service.

It was a short one, but very moving.

When the Earl put the ring on Sadira's finger she could hear once again the angels singing.

She felt too that her mother was near, approving of her marriage.

When it came to the blessing the Earl knelt.

Sadira put her hands together in the age-old gesture of prayer.

She was sure as Father Christopher made the sign of the cross and blessed them that they would be happy.

Their love would deepen as the years passed because it was the love that came from God.

Then, without speaking, Father Christopher left the room.

The Earl put his arms around Sadira.

"My darling, my wife!" he said. "Now you are mine and I will never lose you."

"And I . . . will never . . leave you . . . my wonderful . . . husband," Sadira whispered, "I feel . . . our marriage has . . . united us so . . . closely that we are . . . one person."

"That is exactly what we shall be," the Earl promised.

Then there were no words in which to express what he was feeling. He kissed her until the room swung dizzily round them and they were flying into the sunlit sky.

A little later Father Christopher came back. "Before I leave, My Lady," he said to Sadira, "I want to tell you that your bravery in saving the baby last night has been of immense benefit to me and to all the Christians in Fez."

Sadira looked surprised and he explained, "The child is a Moslem, and because you saved him from certain death the Moslems have asked me to express their gratitude to you."

He paused and then continued, "What is more they have promised to stop their persecution of the Christians in Fez and to try to live beside them amicably."

"I am so glad, Father, so very glad!" Sadira said.

"And so am I, my daughter. At the same time I am sorry to lose my disciple."

"We shall always take an interest in what you are doing, Father," the Earl promised, "and we will come back to see you next year, if you are still here."

"I would like that," Father Christopher said simply, "and I must thank you again, my Lord, for your generous donation towards my cause."

Sadira looked at the Earl and smiled. It was so like him, she thought, to help Father Christopher.

"Now I am leaving you," Father Christopher said, "but I hope I shall see you again before you leave Morocco."

"That may not be possible," the Earl replied. "Sadira has to go home to her father, so we are having only a short honeymoon before we return in my yacht which is in Rabat."

"The Sultan told me that he has lent you his Palace by the sea," Father Christopher said. "It is a very beautiful place which might have been made for honeymooners."

The Earl walked with Father Christopher towards the door. When he was moving down the passage he went back to Sadira. He stood for a moment just looking at her. Then she held out her arms and he threw himself down on the bed beside her.

"I love you! I love you! I love you!" he said. "So much that I am afraid you will grow tired of me telling you so."

"Only if you ... get tired of me ... saying the same thing," Sadira murmured. "Oh, Norwin ... how can ... this have happened?" I was so ... miserable and ... distraught before I left England, and yet now I have ... found the Paradise I longed for here ... in the most ... unlikely

"You will find, my darling, that anywhere is Paradise as long as we are together," the Earl replied, "and that is what I will make it for you."

Then he was kissing her; kissing her so that there was no need for words.

Sadira knew then that they had both found the perfection of love.

It was an inexpressible rapture.

A love that was different from the kind which had shocked and upset her.

She knew that was something which would never trouble them again.

Very much later after she had touched the peaks of ecstasy, she realised she could see the stars.

They covered the sky like sparkling jewels.

"We have both found the flawless stone we longed for," she thought.

Then she remembered it was the stars which had told her to run away. "Thank you, thank you!" she said to them in her heart.

Then the Earl's arms were round her and he drew her close to him. His lips held hers captive and her body, heart and soul quivered with the wonder of it.

It was impossible to think of anything – except him.